EQUIPOISE

EQUIPOISE

KATIE ZDYBEL

singular fiction, poetry, nonfiction, translation, drama, and graphic books

Library and Archives Canada Cataloguing in Publication

Title: Equipoise / Katie Zdybel.
Names: Zdybel, Katie, author.
Identifiers: Canadiana (print) 20210212462 | Canadiana (ebook) 20210212470 |
ISBN 9781550969337 (softcover) | ISBN 9781550969344 (EPUB) |
ISBN 9781550969351 (Kindle) | ISBN 9781550969368 (PDF)
Subjects: LCGFT: Short stories.
Classification: LCC PS8649.D93 E68 2021 | DDC C813/.6—dc23

Copyright © Katie Zdybel, 2021
Book and cover designed by Michael Callaghan
Typeset in Garamond and Jansen Text fonts at Moons of Jupiter Studios
Published by Exile Editions Ltd ~ www.ExileEditions.com
144483 Southgate Road 14 – GD, Holstein, Ontario, N0G 2A0
Printed and Bound in Canada by Imprimerie Gauvin

We gratefully acknowledge the Canada Council for the Arts, the Government of
Canada, the Ontario Arts Council, and Ontario Creates for their support
toward our publishing activities.

Canadian sales representation: The Canadian Manda Group, 664 Annette Street,
Toronto ON M6S 2C8 www.mandagroup.com 416 516 0911

North American and international distribution, and U.S. sales:
Independent Publishers Group, 814 North Franklin Street,
Chicago IL 60610 www.ipgbook.com toll free: 1 800 888 4741

In loving memory of Bunny (Lois) Traines,
an extraordinary woman of great love, strength, and joy.

THE LAST THUNDERSTORM
SWIM OF THE SUMMER

Ginny woke in the passenger seat at a gas station, chin slack, slick of drool. Her mother, Margot, pumping gas. She'd fallen asleep hours ago, hooded sweatshirt wadded between head and car door, hair matted, breath sour. Ginny flipped down the visor mirror, licked a finger, rubbed at mascara adrift in the purple hollows below her eyes. Margot had arrived early at her dorm room, and Ginny had had to claw upward from a royal hangover, flailing sheets aside and shouting through the door that she needed 20 minutes. "Wait for me downstairs!" she commanded, voice a rasp in her throat.

The guy she had met last night was stirring, peeved. He was pulling on jeans, stepping into flip-flops, coaxing his eyes awake with the dull heels of his hands. "Uh, see ya, Jenny," he muttered, half laughing as he lurched to the door. Ginny half-laughed, too – a frog croak. She stood pinching a blanket around her, one hip cocked, "Yeah, see ya," then penguin-shuffled to the mirror to check her reflection. Her concealer had dried on her cheeks in a pattern that looked almost organic, like finely cracked earth.

"Good morning, Sleeping Beauty," Margot said as she nestled back in the driver's seat with two Styrofoam cups of coffee. She had a way of settling into car seats with her butt that Ginny found annoying. "You missed most of the new book."

Margot always listened to audiobooks – books on tape, she still called them – when they drove to the cottage.

Ginny smacked her lips. "Water."

"Behind you. Were you out late last night?"

"Yeah. With the girls." She chugged, then excavated crusts of sleep from her eyes with a pinky fingernail painted vixen violet.

"Which girls?"

"Where are we?"

"I don't know your university friends like I knew your St. Andrew's friends. Do you see them anymore? Lucy? Claire?"

"Where. Are. We?" Ginny repeated slowly.

"We are very close," Margot said, choosing to let it slide. She rolled her window down, exaggerated her inhale. "Smell that air." She had that self-satisfied look she used to have when she'd take Ginny to a pick-your-own apple orchard or a poetry reading.

Ginny turned her head away, letting it fall against the glass and watched the landscape scroll: blasted boulders and pine trees with scab-like bark. The sky thickly grey – a sludgy sponge heavy with dishwater. When she'd last been awake they'd been in central Michigan, past the suburbs of Ann Arbor, where the mustard fields blazed yolk so yellow they stung her eyes. Faded brick farmhouses so ancient and hot with sun she imagined they'd be soft if she touched them, like a tomato left out in the heat.

Then they'd neared the fringe of cottage country (where they usually spent their summers) with its affluent towns all dolled up for tourists – flowers in the front yards like swipes of lipstick and blush, electric purple eyeshadow, glistening in the humidity. Then they'd passed through that familiar territory and carried on north. Here, she saw no houses in any direction and the air smelled like dirty pennies.

Ginny realized she had been hoping her mother was not serious about cottaging somewhere new this August. For the past five years they had been going to a cottage on the west coast of Michigan – the pretty part – in a town that butted up against Sleeping Bear Dunes. They had stayed with Josephine and Cici, and sometimes Mark. But this summer, they were not.

They had long driven past the turnoff for Sleeping Bear Dunes, and were now at the northern crust of Michigan, the Upper Peninsula, or the U.P. as locals called it. When her parents were still together, when she was really young, they'd made the long drive to the Upper Peninsula as a family once. Ginny had forgotten it, but Margot would talk about this area as though it were some sacred wilderness where poems were born.

Ginny roused. "I just don't understand why we aren't going to Josephine and Cici's like normal."

Margot's fingers tripped over the iPod. Ginny leaned forward automatically to press pause for her. "A change of scene is good for the soul," Margot said, once the narrator had gone silent.

"My soul?" Ginny sneered. "It's ugly here."

"Oh, I don't know about that. It's just a different kind of beautiful."

"Great."

Margot blew into her Styrofoam coffee. "You didn't have to come if you didn't want to, dear daughter. You are no man's captive."

Ginny studied her, then looked back out the window. She pictured her mother with her Virginia Woolf and her chamomile tea, alone. "Josephine emailed me, you know. She wants us to come."

Margot's eyes were steady. "Did she now?"

They were curving off the highway onto a pebbly road. It jagged around a sparse stand of pines; stones clacked under tires. Ginny's mother stopped the car when a mud brown cabin with flaking dark green trim appeared in the shadows. Behind the cottage, a grey lake licked a brown teacup rim. Margot was emerging from the car, stretching her arms out, unfurling like a gangly, tall bird – an ostrich or flamingo. She wore a print skirt and it ribboned around her shiny white ankles in the damp wind. There were no other cottages in sight and she turned to Ginny triumphantly: "We have the whole lake to ourselves!"

The first summer Ginny had cottaged at Sleeping Bear Dunes, her father, Eric, had been with them. The dunes were a thousand-foot drop, an almost-vertical cliff of crystalline sand plunging into the turquoise coastline of Lake Michigan. There was something almost tropical, exotic, dangerous about the dunes. Ginny felt like they could have been anywhere: Costa Rica, Treasure Island. She felt magnetized to the cliffs, to the water. She begged her parents to take on the plummet.

They went flying down; mother, father, and daughter – one gangly, six-legged, airborne, newborn insect, striding, landing in the soft sand, their feet sinking as though into warm wax. And with each spring of the knee upward, Ginny sailed a moment, a winged thing, with only shades of Aegean, sapphire, and cerulean beaded in crystal and light, before her. The lake spread out as far as she could see and to each side as far as she could see, and it appeared as though someone had crushed glass and scattered it across the lake's surface so that it blinded her. Every star had been pulled down for her and sewn onto this silk. It was her last happy all-together-family memory.

They swam and then her parents dozed at the edge, their legs tangled together in the water like some kind of iridescent sea plant, their upper bodies beached, sun-burning, vanilla ice cream turning strawberry. Ginny collected delicate violet seashells, small as a baby's pinky toenails, that tinkled together in her palm, calm and sure that life would always be so.

On the ascent Ginny's family met up with the woman two-thirds from the top. (By then they were parched, cramping. It took 10 minutes to fly down, an hour to climb up.) She was alone, and for a moment Ginny saw that her father's gaze was stuck on the perfect behind bobbing its way slowly up the hill. The woman wore a tiny, neon pink bikini and her long, tanned legs were shiny with sweat and oil. Then she turned around and they saw the distress on her face.

"Watch her," Eric called to Margot, who was straggling behind, breathing hard, and he gestured at Ginny. He fumbled up the slope and offered the woman his water, which she took and then immediately passed out. "A little help here!" he called. Ginny watched a chain reaction ripple all the way to the top, where someone used the emergency phone to make the call of the summer.

Ginny learned later that the locals were usually disdainful of those who failed the climb, bristling at the cost to the state and pointing out the clearly posted warning signs, but that year, as the stretcher reached the top with a goddess laid out on it, there was a different reaction. People parted and the emergency team had no trouble getting her into the back of the ambulance. She woke up just then, just as she was about to disappear from view, and the crowd actually cheered. She gave a weak wave – a sassy little salute.

Ginny was hungry and her back felt like it was beginning to burn, but her father insisted they wait.

"Maybe she'll need a ride home or something," he said to Margot.

Ginny's head swivelled from her father to her mother. Her mother was frowning. "I think the emergency team will take care of that."

In the end, Ginny's father won and when the woman was sitting up, chatting with the emergency crew, an ice pack held to her forehead (she made it look jaunty, Ginny thought, like a French beret), he went to her. Ginny stayed with her mom as he leaned his arm against the frame of the ambulance and laughed with the woman. Margot jerked a T-shirt over Ginny's head and nudged her back into her sandals.

They walked behind her father and the woman. Her mom was staring straight ahead; her father was telling a story, his hands moving in a wild, unfamiliar way, and the woman was laughing a deep, head-thrown-back laugh. Her hair swished along her shoulder blades, the blonde highlights darting like silver minnows in dark water. Ginny was stuck on the muscles in the woman's back – delicate, but firm, such a pretty curve to the shoulders. She'd never noticed these on women before. Then again, she'd never seen a woman so naked before, unless you counted the senior citizens in the pool locker room – which she did not, suddenly. She'd seen her mother naked, but Ginny's mother had almost pinky-white skin, the colour left from a pencil eraser rubbed on paper, and no hint of the hot, charged energy this woman's taut arms and legs promised.

The woman was walking smoothly along, her hips sliding as though they were fastened with honey. Her mother, beside Ginny, seemed to be staring at the single, loose knot, holding up the woman's bikini top.

Ginny had been watching her mother watch the woman, when she suddenly felt violently nauseous. Her mouth surged with saliva; someone was squeezing the inside of her head. She wheeled to the side and vomited along the trail that led to the parking lot. Margot snapped to action, rubbing her back and herding her toward a garbage can. Ginny started to cry and whispered, "I want Dad."

Margot shouted to her husband: "She wants you, Eric. Let's get to the car and you can sit with her in the back."

"No, I'll drive, hon." He smiled an I've-got-this-under-control smile, glancing at the woman. The woman turned and seemed to notice Margot and Ginny for the first time – as though Eric had failed to mention them. From the side, Ginny could almost see one of her big, tanned breasts in the full. The shape of a nipple protruding like a little green pea made Ginny feel funny again. She tucked her head against her mother.

"But of course," the woman said. She had a creamy accent that made the words sound like a song. "She wants her father. We women will ride in the front so she can sit with you." And she put her hand on Ginny's father's arm to steer him back toward his puking daughter and, remarkably, he moved in that direction and Margot stepped forward to walk with the woman. She extended her hand: "Josephine," she said. "I have a daughter, Cici." Then she smiled at Ginny, soothing as a nurse. "Just about your age."

Ginny held her cell phone to her ear and marched to the lake shore. Reception was swampy.

"Thank God," she said as her friend answered. "Ceese, it's freaking freezing here. I'm wearing a sweater."

"Like a cotton sweater or wool?"

"Wool, Cici! It's not, like, a cool evening at the beach; it feels like winter."

"Then get down here."

Ginny slapped a mosquito against her thigh and it belched blood. "I can't. My mom would be all alone."

Margot came out wearing her ratty bathrobe. "I'm jumping in!" she called. "You brave enough to join me?"

"No, thanks."

"Well, I'm going for it." She flung her robe to the rock below her and, after surveying the water, took a flailing leap from the lip of the rock, screaming as she flew through the air, her body all cocked angles and crooked lines in the moment before she plunged below the surface.

Ginny went to the cottage with Cici still on the line, and found some potato chips to lick the salt from. When she glanced back out the window, she saw her mom floating on her back in the water, kicking her pale legs out like a water strider to skim along the surface.

Ginny huffed. "You're so lucky. Your mom would never drag you to a place like this. Your mom's cool."

Cici just laughed. "Whatever. Moms are moms."

"Yeah, but you know what I mean. My mom's practically a spinster, I swear. I mean, I know what she'll want to do all weekend – play Scrabble and watch movies from the eighties."

"I thought you liked that."

"Yeah, when I was 15. I want to go out, have a drink, you know what I mean."

Cici was quiet on the line.

"I mean, I'm in university now. I'm not some little girl in braids making brownies with my mom on a Friday night. I bet you and your mom can swap clothes, go out for cosmos together, that kind of thing. My mom is always thinking of the educational angle, I swear. You know what she asked me to do with her last weekend? March in a parade for equal pay or something."

"We don't wear the same clothes," Cici said.

Cici had made a scrapbook for Ginny last year, for her 18th birthday. Photographs of the two of them as young teens in their swimsuits on the beach by the cottage. There was a photo of their mothers standing knee-deep in the water, marinating in discussion. Margot with her long, dull, brown hair that swelled in the humidity and lay limp the rest of the time. She wore it in two braids down her back. Her paper-bag brown eyes disappeared into her face, thin lips revealed slightly crooked canines the colour of old pearls. Maybe if she wore makeup, Ginny thought. Josephine, on the other hand, looked stunning. She wore a Bond girl red bikini with the side buckle and oversized Jackie O. sunglasses and lipstick the colour and shine of a race car.

After their first meeting, Josephine and Margot exchanged numbers and had kept in touch, then, when the next summer rolled around, Josephine called to ask Margot if they were coming back to Sleeping Bear Dunes.

"Come stay with us. We have this giant castle and Mark is never here. It's just Cici and me and I get lonely. Come. Please."

Margot had had to explain that she and Eric were going through a separation.

"All the more reason to come," was Josephine's reply.

That was the first of five Augusts which Margot and Ginny spent with Josephine and Cici, and sometimes Mark, in the big cottage by Sleeping Bear Dunes. Ginny thought it was good for her mom, an English professor at York University, who could be addicted to her books and was often frustrated with her attempts at poetry, to be around new people. Josephine often had other friends over for drinks on the deck or got Margot dressed up in her vibrant clothing and took her out to one of the town bars, leaving the girls to watch movies and eat ice cream at the cottage. Ginny could see them now getting ready up in Josephine's bedroom: Margot had a way of buttoning up what Josephine would leave undone, or pulling a cardigan over a low-cut tank top. Then Josephine would study her and say, generously, "Much better. Maybe just a pair of earrings." And Margot would wear them and act a bit differently – sillier or younger, Ginny thought. Like she was playing dress-up.

Over the years, Josephine had introduced Margot to plenty of decent, age-appropriate men. She'd find some reason why a couple of guys should stop by, just a quick hello, a chance to see the woodwork inside the beautiful cottage, and Ginny would feel fizz in her body those evenings as though something wonderfully, terrifyingly grown-up might happen.

Ginny remembered the men: tanned and eager to make the women laugh, thirsty for a drink. She'd watch Josephine introduce them to Margot and then she'd watch the men orbit Josephine, in a sheer dress with a slit up to there, for the rest of the night. Josephine always shone, but she was a supernova in a crowd. After trying to drum up some deeper conversation, Margot seemed relieved to be left on the sidelines, nibbling on the olives from her drink, observing. Ginny, watching with Cici from the upstairs landing, would see her mother standing alone and feel the fizz go flat. It was replaced with a strange cocktail of things: disappointment, relief, something like pride, and something like loneliness – the kind you feel in your own body so that another person doesn't have to.

One night at the cottage, Ginny was awakened by a thunderstorm. A rumble of thunder came up so sudden and deep that Ginny felt it bang on the drum of her stomach. Another flash: she rolled out of bed, slid to the window. The entire, great black body of water flashed white – as though a giant light bulb under the surface had been switched on. The power and the beauty of those storms! Light came again, a magnificent bolt lighting up the dark clouds in the black sky above and skittering down in a thick, crooked vein of sheer white energy. It illuminated the beach, where Ginny saw Margot and Josephine, shimmering there at the edge of the fierce waves, their clothes thrown to the sand, jumping back with glee when the water swelled unexpectedly and threatened to swallow them, the air around crackling with electricity. A sonic boom strummed every nerve in Ginny's body; she was a tuning fork, struck and vibrating.

"Let's have some tea and play Scrabble," said Margot, slick as an otter and breathless from her swim. Ginny was curled up on the couch in the living room, thumbing through texts on her phone.

"This couch is scratchy."

"Are you tired? Are you sure you don't want to jump in the lake? It might refresh you."

Ginny watched her mom fish their old game box out of her embroidered bag and plop it on the table. She had pulled a T-shirt over her head which read NICE WOMEN DON'T MAKE HISTORY. (Ha, Ginny thought. Her mom was the epitome of nice.) She opened cupboard doors looking for mugs, found two, rinsed them out. "Go ahead, Ginny. Have a swim. I'll wait," she said over her shoulder.

"Obviously," Ginny said, only half-meaning for her mom to hear.

But Margot did. She filled an electric kettle with water from the tap. "Obviously what?"

"Well, who else are you going to wait for?"

Margot just looked at her.

"I mean, if you want to play a game, what other option have you got?"

After her parents' divorce, Ginny and Margot had moved into a two-bedroom apartment on York campus. On the first night, though she knew she was too old for it, Ginny dragged her sleeping bag and pillow into her mom's room and curled up on the floor, hoping.

"Come on up here, Virginia Woolf," her mom had said, waking in the night and seeing her there.

From that night, Ginny would arrive in her mother's doorway, wait for her mom to pat the bed beside her. She'd fall asleep to the sound of her mother reading to her, the crown of her head snug in her mother's armpit. (She smelled like Dove soap.) Her mother never asked her to go to her own bed and even when she was in her teens, she'd wake up with her mother's arm slung across her chest, the feeling of being loved, a sewn together, warm, sleepy thing.

Ginny had gone to an all-girls private school, kindergarten through grade 12. She had liked it. Liked her blue and green plaid uniform skirt, liked the sharp lemon smell of the shiny floors, liked Mr. Kerr, her English teacher. She'd been good at math in the beginning; her dad said she took after him. Margot would make jokes, soft ones, about losing Ginny to the dark side. She'd read poems to Ginny and it became a ritual, a comic routine, between the two of them: Ginny's raised eyebrows and shaking head, like nope. Makes no sense. Margot would clap the book shut and peer into her daughter, feign deep disappointment. "Really? Not even Whitman? Oh! How can my own flesh and blood not be moved to thrills by the body electric?" They would laugh – they knew how to lean into each other and laugh back then, at all things that were out of place for them, a mother and daughter on their own, no man in the house, no nuclear family shape to their life. Then, around the end of high school, it was like the tidal change of hormones swept in a new brain chemistry. She hated math, found it frustrating, pointless – and started liking poetry.

She hid it, and hid from it, at first. Mr. Kerr assigned them a poem to write and she'd scoffed, spent her weekend on a biology project, then late Sunday night, snapped a piece of blank paper onto her desk in her mint green bedroom, clicked her Hello Kitty pen and started writing. Almost immediately something began to trickle out of her that she had not known she contained. It was like some part of her had been incubating for years, waiting for this silly little assignment.

She wrote a poem. A decent one. She liked it. She pushed back from the desk. Her mother wrote poems. Not her. She was math and science, field hockey, boy bands; read fast-paced, addictive, flashy young adult novels. She didn't like the poems her mom read to her.

But then, she did. It hit her like how a wave washes over you, shockingly, all-consuming in its slosh, tipping your centre of gravity. She realized she had come to crave those moments when her mother read strangeness to her, a scant, holy paragraph flashing gauzy images through her mind like sheets rising and snapping on a clothesline. A picture slowly appearing as on a Polaroid, the tones all brownish-yellowish, edges hazed.

She began trickling poems on the regular, tucking them inside her biology textbook when her mother walked by her bedroom. (Mr. Kerr, the English teacher, was devouring them. "You're a regular Margot Pearson," he said, full of praise. "Your mother must be so pleased.") Then the last year of high school was over and it was time to go to university. Life sprinted. She was out of her mom's apartment and into a dorm room with a roommate who blared Beyoncé, seemed 30 to Ginny's 18, and was alarmed that Ginny hadn't had sex yet. "Like 100 per cent virgin?" She asked. ("Just 27.3 per cent," Ginny wanted to say, but recognized she was now in a situation where she was suddenly uncool and had to watch her words.)

The other girls in her dorm had serious boyfriends, or sometimes girlfriends, who they'd had all kinds of sex with or they were dramatically, heart-wrenchingly, breaking up with because they were throwing themselves into some hot and messy thing with someone they'd just met at school. Ginny's friends back at St. Andrew's, her all-girls school, were far less experienced. They'd been into sleepovers with Rice Krispie squares studded with gummy bears, recording themselves singing Taylor Swift songs on Garage Band. At university, some of the girls had done things Ginny thought only girls on TV shows set in California did – blow jobs in the bathrooms at bars, threesomes, kissing other girls just to try it.

Ginny hadn't even talked much about boys with Margot. Neither of them dated, really. Ginny had had a couple crushes, and that had been enough to sustain her until now. Watching her roommate stuff condoms into her purse before heading out to a party, Ginny felt a cramp of anger toward her mom that at first she couldn't name.

But the cramp sometimes turned into an ache: she was suddenly surrounded by girls her own age who it seemed were far more experienced in everything, but these girls didn't love their mothers the way Ginny loved hers, she could tell. Didn't cuddle into them anymore, didn't know their smells anymore. Their mothers didn't swing their daughters' legs up onto their laps while they read e. e. cummings in a voice a girl could crawl into, like a tiny thing sheltered in the down of a milkweed pod.

About the time she moved into the dorm, she'd had a conversation with her dad that she'd found hard to forget. He'd had a series of girlfriends, nothing too serious, and he worked downtown for an insurance company, which he loathed. This was his third career change since Ginny's childhood.

She saw him once a week; that had been the arrangement, and he'd always honoured it. Both she and her mom recognized that consistency for what it was: his only one.

He'd taken her shopping for dorm room accoutrements: throw pillows, potted plants, a plug-in kettle. (It had been fun, she and her dad gliding around on a shopping cart in the big-box store, suggesting ridiculous items to each other: "You need a bunion remover? A sparkly hula hoop? Bladder pan?" "Da-ad," she'd wailed gleefully.) They arrived back at her dorm room after burgers at their favourite steakhouse (a place Margot would never go to) their bellies full, still lobbing teasing remarks at each other.

"This is interesting," her dad said, pausing at the doorway of her dorm room where a life-sized poster of Britney Spears at her pigtailed, belly-button-baring peak gazed at them from under drooping eyelids. Ginny, distracted, didn't answer.

"Isn't that a little anti-feminist for you? I mean, I always thought you and your mom were two peas in a pod in that regard. Not interested in catering to that kind of form and all that." Her dad stood scratching his neck, still examining the poster.

Ginny looked up. "Oh. That's my roommate's. She says Britney is her hero."

Her dad gave a confused, slightly concerned laugh. "Explain, please."

"I think she means it ironically. Sort of like a younger Madonna figure, except we all know how Britney turned out. She wasn't afraid to, you know, look like that, do…what she does, but then she crashed and burned – I think that's supposed to be ultra-feminist, or like ironic-feminist. You know, how like people triumph sex workers now." She jumped up suddenly and swung the door so that Britney was left thrusting her exposed hips out to the hallway.

"Uh-huh," Eric said, his eyes now roving the roommate's half of the room.

Ginny turned slowly, mulling, going quiet. "What do you mean, 'not interested in catering to that kind of form?'"

"Oh, you know." Eric picked up a textbook from the roommate's desk and turned it over, scanned the back. "Like you don't try to be all flashy, like a Britney." He held up the book. "Women's Studies?"

"What do you mean 'flashy?' Like…pretty?"

"What?" Eric glanced up, saw Ginny's face. "No, of course not. I mean, you don't try overly hard. You're more natural, like your mom. You're beautiful, Hon."

Not *trying overly hard* could mean she was a sloth, Ginny thought. But said: "You have to say I'm beautiful because I'm your daughter."

"I don't have to say anything. I do really think you're beautiful, Ginny. I have since the moment you were born."

Ginny felt her throat thickening. She slumped onto the edge of her bed, something bubbling over. "I'm dumpy," she said softly. "And plain."

"Feminine," Eric said, crossing the room and putting an arm around her in one quick motion. "And natural. Where's all this coming from?"

Ginny blinked her eyes rapidly. "Dad, why'd you leave Mom?"

His head reeled back. "Wow. Curveball, Ginny." He scratched his neck. "Is this what's really bothering you?"

Ginny wasn't sure, but she nodded vigorously, sniffled.

Eric looked panicked for a moment, then let out a rush of air and shrugged, stared at a spot on the beige carpet.

"I don't know, Ginny. It's complex. I guess…if I'm honest…I don't know, somewhere along the line, I stopped being attracted to her."

Ginny flinched. You never want to hear your parents talking about sex, even a lack thereof.

At first she thought that it didn't make any difference to her. But then she found herself replaying what her dad had said in her head, often. It was uncomfortable – like a scab she'd picked, almost by accident, and now she had to suffer the rawness of the wound underneath. There'd been a time when she had felt protective of her mother, stung, on her behalf, by her dad's departure. Slowly, that sting turned into something else. Embarrassment maybe.

On weekends, when Mark, Josephine's husband, came to the cottage at Sleeping Bear Dunes, the first thing he would do was pour himself a drink. Scotch on ice. The mossy smell of it still made Ginny think of the shift in the house when he arrived. Mark added a certain measure of structure that the mothers didn't necessarily adhere to when he wasn't there. Meals would happen around normal meal times, for example. Their mothers would become more attentive, instead of being mostly in their world of two, giggling, engrossed in conversations that were just a bit too low to hear. And they were less likely to run to the water in the middle of the night when Mark was around.

Mark had a soft paunch, a dignified face. He was much older than Josephine. He taught economics at the University of Michigan in Ann Arbor. When he first arrived he would look at his wife in a hungry way, as though he had just seen her for the first time. Ginny sometimes watched with discomfort and sometimes with fascination, but he would be restrained and stay downstairs to ask Margot how her drive was and hear about the girls' adventures. Josephine would be cooking and not talking for once, letting everyone else chat, then she would walk slyly by Mark with a platter of food in her hand and brush against him, or lean down low over him and ask if he would like some.

Later, when Ginny was older, she watched this mating ritual in a more studious way. How Josephine made him wait. Just when Mark would stand up, stretch, and announce he'd had a long day, a tiring drive, she'd suggest they all go to the porch to watch the sunset and Mark would always concede. And then the drinks would stretch out longer than the sunset, and she would notice outside that Josephine's dress was sheer and she smelled sweaty in a good way, like spices in a dark restaurant, and she was sitting so close to Margot, turning to whisper something in her ear, moving Margot's hair aside gently, and then laughing privately, and then all of a sudden Mark would just stand up and go inside, and Josephine would set her drink down and follow him, a little smile pulling at the corner of her lips. Ginny could still remember the feeling of watching Josephine slide that piece of hair behind her mother's ear. She could feel it – the tip of Josephine's long fingernail against the smooth, sensitive skin behind her ear and it made her shiver.

The next morning, Mark came down spritely, refreshed. Margot already up, the early bird of the cottage, and she and Mark would start talking about writers they both admired or the politics of a university career, and it would pick up speed like a tennis match, this conversation, volleying back and forth, with only the sound of Josephine, once she woke later, in the kitchen, whacking a spatula against a frying pan or kicking the fridge door shut with the heel of her sandal.

The next morning, Ginny slept until 11. When she shuffled out to the living room, Margot was just coming in from outside. She had on a shapeless, dark brown rain jacket with the hood up; her hair was wet around the edges and frizzing as though she were wearing a bird's nest for a cap. She carried a soggy paper bag of groceries with a box of Cap'n Crunch peeping from the top.

"Mom, I don't eat that anymore. Too many calories. I want to go to Sleeping Bear Dunes."

Margot froze mid-unzipping. "Well, I had a good sleep, thanks. And you?"

Ginny knotted her arms over her chest.

Margot was pulling items out of the grocery bag, slowly, carefully. "You can go if you want to."

"No, I can't," Ginny said. "Then you'll be here all alone."

Margot turned around at this. "I have no problem being alone," she said.

Ginny shook her head. "Sure," she said under breath, then jumped up, stomped into her room, began picking up the clothes she had flung out of her duffel bag the night before. She folded them in one at a time, glancing into the living room.

"Okay, I'm going," she said a few minutes later, her bag slung over her shoulder. "I'm going down to Cici and Josephine's."

Margot sat on a musty plaid couch on the screened-in porch, reading Jan Zwicky. "Drive safely."

Ginny felt a little fountain-like surge of annoyance. "I wish you hadn't dragged me up here. I should have just gone straight there and not wasted two whole days." She was surprised at a small choke in her voice. It made her sound angrier, or more hurt, than she meant to.

Margot neatly placed a worn bookmark between two pages and looked at her daughter.

Ginny put a hand on one hip. "And what? You're just going to sit here and read books all August? By yourself?"

Margot was looking at her, calm as milk. "I have some planning to do, actually, for one of my courses. Don't worry about me."

"I'm not."

"Very good."

"Okay. Fine. Then I'm going."

Margot took a deep breath. "Virginia," she said, and Ginny thought, *Now she's going to let me have it,* but Margot said evenly, "You must make your own choices."

Ginny blinked. That's it? She hesitated a fraction then whirled around. "I don't want to stay up here with you because it'll be too boring. At least Josephine is an interesting person." The flash of satisfaction gave way almost immediately to a horrible, sickening clot of phlegm that took great effort to swallow. She hurried to the driveway. For some reason, at that moment, she recalled the sensation of leaning against her mom's shoulder when she was in a deep laugh, the warm vibration of it, the hum. She decided it was better to not look back when her mom said: "I'm here if you should change your mind."

As Ginny drove the four hours down to Sleeping Bear Dunes, the sickening feeling hardened and sharpened. The further she drove from her mother, the easier it became to be angry at her. She felt charged, hurried. A storm was rolling in over the lake and she left the window down, let it whip her hair in lashes.

Her body had changed this year; a conscious need to break from the past. She'd taken up Zumba, ate sparingly, trying to carve out a new figure. One that she believed would make her feel differently about herself. And, to her surprise, it had worked. She felt attractive for the first time – it was an exciting, powerful feeling – sometimes a bit unwieldy. A few months ago she'd noticed guys were looking at her. From there, it was simple. Flirting tumbled so quickly into making out, which hurtled – she was surprised to discover – into sex, if she wanted it. And she did, mostly. She was amazed at how something she'd thought was so elusive was actually too effortless. She'd had sex with four different guys now, each one a little easier than the last.

It was late when she got to Cici and Josephine's cottage and she found Cici on the couch eating a bowl of ice cream.

"I thought we were going out," Ginny said. She hadn't even set her bag down yet. She'd get like this sometimes now, her body vibrant, impatient.

"I thought you'd be tired."

"Come on, Cici."

After tugging on a dress and smearing on some lipstick, she was just about ready. Cici came into the bathroom in a pair of jeans with holes in the knees and a tank top that she had twisted in a knot at one hip. Ginny glanced back at her own reflection and applied mascara until it looked like broken insect legs were stuck to her lashes.

"You're dressed up," Cici remarked.

When they reached the front door of the bar, they had to pass through a tight cluster of guys with baseball caps and pre-faded jeans. "Hey there," one of them said to Cici as they passed. Cici glared at him. Ginny tossed him a look over her shoulder, dropping it so that the strap of her dress would fall as she knew it would. Felt a little current run through her. Cici pulled her strap back into place for her.

They had just started on their beers when the guy from outside came shouldering his way toward their table, a friend in tow.

He pulled a chair up without asking and looked back and forth between Cici and Ginny.

"So," he said and grinned.

Ginny smiled back. "Who's your friend?" she asked. She said this at the exact time Cici said, "Do you mind?"

He looked at Cici. "Sorry. Is this a private conversation?"

Ginny leaned forward. "Maybe it is." Then remembering the way Josephine always did it, leaned back again and looked away, as though she had better things to do.

Cici wasn't having any of it. "Look, I'm out for a drink with my friend. I don't know where you guys rolled in from, but—"

"Lansing," he answered. "Just for the weekend." He was good-looking in an unexciting way – nice build, planned amount of stubble. "My friend here is Cody. I'm Kyle."

"Excellent." Cici rolled her eyes at Ginny. "Think you could leave us alone now?"

Kyle pulled his hands back from the table and held them up. "Hey, okay, if that's what you want. I'll see you guys later," and he winked at Ginny before moving back into the crowd.

"Cute," Ginny said to Cici.

"Cocky. He thinks he doesn't even have to try."

"So? What else are people here for? He's just cutting to the chase."

"Some people are here for the music – or the company."

Ginny laughed. "Yeah, right," she said, catching Kyle's eye as he slid onto a stool across the room.

Cici stood abruptly. "I'm going to the bathroom."

Ginny took a swig of her drink and made herself look away from Kyle, though she could feel his eyes on her. This was the crucial part, she'd learned, look just interested enough, not too much. A few minutes later, Kyle was in Cici's chair.

"Hey, Ceese," Ginny said, her voice a little silkier than usual, when her friend returned. "Want to go to a party?"

"We just got here."

"Kyle wants to show us his place."

Cici looked away. "You know what? You go. I'm going home."

"Ceese," Kyle said in a pretend pleading tone, and Ginny giggled.

Cici glowered at him, then looked at Ginny. "Can I talk to you in private for a sec?"

Kyle raised his brow and he and Ginny exchanged glances. "I think I'm in trouble," Ginny mouthed at him and lurched a bit as she stood. She had opted for high-heeled sandals instead of flip-flops.

They stepped away from the table and Cici leaned close so Ginny could hear her without shouting. "What's gotten into you? I thought you wanted to go out and have a drink – we haven't seen each other in forever. This guy's a total frat boy. He just wants to get laid and then forget you."

Ginny could feel Kyle's stare and she turned so that her ass was sticking out, with the skirt creeping up her legs. "I'll catch up with you later."

"What?" Cici shook her head; she couldn't hear her. The band had just kicked it up a notch. Ginny looked over her shoulder. Kyle was looking at her, not at Cici but at her. The way Mark used to stare at Josephine when they'd be out on the deck, watching the sunset. She could make him keep waiting, or she could make it fast. Ginny pressed herself close to Cici and slowly moved a piece of hair that had escaped her friend's ponytail. She leaned in to whisper something, but Cici jumped back.

"What are you doing? God, Ginny."

Ginny felt her stomach drop sharply. "I'm sorry," she said quickly, and meant it, but Cici was shaking her head, her eyes hard.

"What's with the new look, Ginny? It's a bit obtuse, you know. I mean, there's nothing wrong with rocking a mini-skirt, but don't do it for that loser – or any other guy."

"I'm sorry, Cici, I just thought—"

Cici shot her an incredulous look. "I know what you thought. You'd go home with him? Some stranger? Seriously, Ginny, what's gotten into you? I mean, if this is what you're going for these days, I'm out."

Ginny opened her mouth, but didn't know what to say. Cici, of all people wielded the power to get any guy whenever she wanted to. Or so she thought. But now that Ginny thought about it, Cici didn't talk about sleeping with guys much. She'd had a serious boyfriend for a while, then nothing. The band suddenly shot into high gear. "I don't know how to do this!" Ginny shouted.

Cici was shaking her head, pointing to her ear. "Can't hear you," she mouthed.

The music swelled even louder; Ginny knew it would swallow her words. "I wasn't ready. Everybody else was just doing it whenever, like no big deal. I didn't know what I was doing! My mom didn't, like, prepare me. Didn't show me how you're supposed to be with guys." She kept yelling, knowing Cici couldn't hear her. She shook her head thinking of what she had known: the crackle off her body, intensity reflected in their stares, urgent playfulness, then the feeling of waking up in the morning, the electricity lost. Embarrassment.

The crescendo of music relented. There was a vacuum of quiet in the bar. Cici was still looking at her, watching her mouth.

"You're just doing it for the wrong reasons," she said, after a moment. She turned to go, then looked back at Ginny, her face stern.

A flash of lightning woke Ginny a few hours later. She rolled over in bed to see Cici, still dressed and on top of the sheets, asleep with her arm pillowed under her head. They'd fallen asleep talking.

Ginny went to the window as a great pop lit the sky. In its flash, she saw Josephine in one of the Adirondacks by the water, alone. She hesitated, then went to the door, walked through the dark cottage hallway, down the stairs.

Ginny felt a vibrating growl of thunder as she stood at the screen door, looking out at Josephine's silhouette. She felt nervous suddenly, but couldn't name why. It seemed important to talk to Josephine, right now, though she couldn't think of any logical reason for it. She sucked in a breath, walked across the wet sand. The air was thick with humidity.

"Do you want a drink?" Josephine asked as Ginny approached, and then without waiting for her response pushed a plastic wine glass into Ginny's hand. "Come. Talk to me." She gestured at the other chair. "I'm glad you came to the cottage. I haven't been good company for Cici. Mark has been cheating on me. I may have to leave him. Cecilia doesn't know yet."

Ginny froze with her hand reaching for the pitcher. "What?" She was suddenly acutely aware of everything. The cluster of gnats around the porch light. The smell of jasmine in the perfume that Josephine wore. A curl of wave spiraling down hard into the sand at the water's edge before collapsing.

Josephine shuffled in her blanket. Her face looked tired, sculptural, her long hair snaking around her face.

"It's someone at the university. A professor of literature." She said *literature* in a fake British accent, slow and with her deep voice. Then laughed roughly; a vapour of vodka rose from her mouth. "Of course."

Ginny swallowed, not sure what to say, and feeling meek, asked: "Do you think you can work it out?"

Josephine gave her a hard look. "How do I work that out?" She snorted. "And why should I?" She took a long drink. "One thing you need to know, Ginny, about men. One thing I can tell you." She was a bit slurry, but she looked Ginny in the eye steadily. "It's not enough to attract them. They might think so at first, but they want more. The whole package. And you know what else? If you think sex might trump everything else, which you might," and her drink came smacking down, slopping over the edge, "it doesn't." She took another slurp. "What does he mean, he wants someone he can really talk to? I can talk!" She looked at Ginny. "I am the whole fucking package. He just never seemed interested in what I had to say." And then she was quiet for a long time and Ginny sat awkwardly, wishing she could get out of the chair and crawl into her mother's bed.

"Your mom and I could talk a blue streak," Josephine said, as though Ginny's thought had been aloud. Josephine held up her glass and aimed her pointer finger at Ginny. "I was always trying to figure out from your mother how to be alone so well. I mean, how to be alone and like it. It's a very attractive quality."

"It is?"

"Oh, very."

Ginny didn't know what to say.

Josephine studied her, a skeptical look creeping over her face. "I don't know what I'd do without Cici."

Ginny felt a seasick sensation in her stomach and closed her eyes. If she could just be transported back to her mom's room tonight she'd apologize for everything, stop sleeping with guys she barely knew, she'd start writing poems again, and this time she would read them to her mother.

"Let's go for a swim!" Josephine cried. "Come. Look at those waves. Let's have a thunderstorm swim. Last one of the summer." She stood up and peeled back her silk robe, revealing a black bikini underneath.

"I don't have my bathing suit on," Ginny said dumbly. Josephine just grabbed her hand and pulled her. They went running across the wet sand and towards the waves, black in the night, and Josephine plunged in without slowing down, dragging Ginny with her. She wasn't ready for it and the waves had a pull to them and she sucked in water and came up choking. Josephine was already back under, her bathing suit off, her naked body rising to the moon. Ginny spat water, gasping. She grasped for her bearing, then found a small centre of gravity.

She took a deep breath and dove under, peeling her dress off in one motion, feeling the cool flow of water over her naked body and pulling with her arms, kicking so that she went out farther. She came up triumphantly, turned to face Josephine.

"There's nothing like this!" Josephine shouted to her. "Swimming naked in a storm." Then she laughed, her body shiny, reflecting the flickering light in the sky. Ginny saw something she had never seen before: the power and the beauty of a woman's body – not as a way of attracting men, but just as a way of being, in its own right. She plunged back down, grabbing a fistful of sand and using it to scrub her face clean. The way she and Cici had done years before, giddily explaining to their mothers that they were exfoliating – back when that was a new, funny word to them. Back when there was nothing to scrape off.

THE LIFEBOATS

We are upstairs at the Thurbers' house. My sister, Layla, and I have been tasked with watching our little brother and Phoebe Thurber, while the adults eat crackers with pâté and drink coffee downstairs.

Phoebe says, "Let's push the beds together and pretend we're on the back of a whale, swimming out to sea."

Layla and I look at each other. I think about saying it's not a good idea, but Phoebe and Paul have already begun the work of tightening their little bodies against the bed frames, inching them across the wood floor. Layla joins them, her eyes still on mine. We will play whatever Phoebe wants today, her look seems to say.

"And it's night-time and there's a storm and we need our lanterns," Phoebe goes on, plodding across the pillows with her arm held up high, a creaking, imaginary, silver lantern swaying from her small fist. She pauses with one foot on the headboard, her free hand coming to her brow as she squints out across her bedroom.

"Sailor Paul," she commands, "pass me my telescope. I think I see something in the water."

"Phoebe—" I begin, but she cuts me off.

"It's *Captain*. I'm the captain, now."

My little brother, looking fearful, scurries to her with the water glass from the bedside table in his hand.

Layla joins them at the headboard and I frown at her. I hear the dull tones of adult conversation through the floorboards, the flat clink of silverware on plates.

"Let's play something else," I say.

"Don't," Layla says to me.

Phoebe holds up the water glass, her face scrunched around it, searching the sea, then she looks down at Paul. "It's a grown-up."

I'm across the room in a second. "Come on now, Phoebe—"

"Captain," all three say at once. I pull my hand back and look at them.

From downstairs, half a phrase, a flotsam of discussion floats upward: *"...how children cope with it."*

Phoebe throws down her glass; it lands with a soft thump on the bedspread. "Quick, Paul! The lifeboats! Lower the lifeboats!"

Paul's nose is pink and watery at the edges – a sign that his world of warm blankets and Mom's lap and bananas with milk in a cream-coloured cup is being tilted.

I hear from downstairs: *"Could it have been an accident?"*

"Layla, please," I hiss and lean to scoop up Paul. "I'm going downstairs and I think you should all stop playing this game."

"If you don't get on the whale, you'll be drownded," Phoebe says. She is solemn.

Paul sniffles, but leans away from me. "I want to stay on the whale."

"It's not a real whale," I tell him.

"Stop it," Layla snaps at me.

I whirl around to face her. "What's the matter with you?"

Layla's nostrils flare. I remember being younger, when Lay and I were Phoebe and Paul's age, how we got caught up in a game, pretending we were mermaids, swimming the corridor between our house and the fence, pretending it was a river, how we crossed into the Thurbers' yard and drifted into the garage, by accident.

We had never been in the garage before. We'd only been through the living room and into the kitchen with Mrs. Thurber where she made coffee for Mom, where they turned the radio on and laughed as they talked. Mrs. Thurber smoked cigarettes that smelled like mints and mothballs. Once we overheard Mom say that Mrs. Thurber was a spirited woman who had been forced into a bad situation. We had tried teasing out what that meant.

Mrs. Thurber worked in a ladies' clothing store downtown, but only two afternoons a week because Mr. Thurber had a job that paid for the big house and boat and car and Phoebe's scalloped yellow coat with the rabbit's fur around the neck. Mrs. Thurber wore cherry pink lipstick and heels that clicked on the sidewalks when we saw her in town, but at home her lips were wiped colourless and she buttoned her cardigan as high it would go.

Another time we heard Mrs. Thurber say that despite all he'd done, she still loved Phoebe's father. This confused me – I wondered why wouldn't she love Mr. Thurber. Layla said, maybe Phoebe's dad is a different man; but I said no way, we'd lived next door to the Thurbers forever and I'd never seen any other man come to visit Phoebe. Not once.

We must be extra kind to Phoebe and help out Mrs. Thurber as much as we can, Mom and Dad had told us many times.

"The lifeboats are ready," Layla says to Phoebe. She pulls Paul into her lap and the three of them face the same direction. For a moment, there is a feeling of tipping and I clutch at the side of the bed.

"Get on the whale, Jody!" Paul yelps at me.

Once we realized we were in the garage we stopped our game. It smelled funny in there – not garage funny, but like smells we weren't used to in our home. In fact, it was nothing like our garage. Where the bicycles and plastic pool and rubber boots should have been was an old, mustard-yellow armchair and a rug. There was a portable television on a piano stool, and a beaten-up wardrobe to the side. The wardrobe door was not quite closed and Layla was there before I even knew it, opening it and leaning back to take in the rows of glittering bottles, filled with brown or clear liquid.

I pulled on her arm and said I wanted to go. The mustard chair had dark spots on the arms, like things had been spilled and not properly cleaned up. Its seat sagged; there was a shadowed indentation in the middle. It seemed like it was waiting for Mr. Thurber, that softened, dark dent, and made me feel that he was somehow here, in the garage with us, like he could materialize at any moment.

I did not want to see Mr. Thurber sitting in that chair, watching the little television. I could picture his flat grey eyes, blank as coins, staring at nothing, the loose, yellowish skin of his arms wrinkled and limp, like a balloon with the air let out.

He looked this way whenever we saw him at the Thurbers' house. Sitting, staring. He wouldn't even say hello. Mrs. Thurber would say, "Go on up to Phoebe's room. Mr. Thurber is watching his program." And she and Mom would go into the kitchen and empty a box of Peek Freans onto a plate for us, the kind with the frilled edges and sugared ruby jam in the middle. Once, I nibbled all the way around the edges of the cookie and stuck its sticky red heart on my throat like a jewel. It suddenly seemed strange to me that she called him that – Mr. Thurber – when Mom called our dad Roger or Rodge or Dear.

There is a heavy thunk from downstairs that makes the floor push up under my feet slightly, and I know the back door has been shut hard. From where I stand, I can see out the window to the back, and I see Mrs. Thurber almost running along the garden path. When she gets to the end, she lights a cigarette and blows a great puff of smoke in the cold air.

Two adults have moved closer to the bottom of the stair-case: *"No one who grew up on the water like he did couldn't have handled those waves."*

"Unless he was—"

"Well, of course."

"He'd had an eye on her forever, that's what I heard. And so when everything happened to her – and he with all his money. I heard him say once he was waiting for her to get used to him."

There's a pause and then the other voice says: *"Almost makes you sorry for him."*

"Makes me sorrier for her."

There's a sudden pitching feeling and my stomach feels sea-sick. I wonder about Mrs. Thurber. I wonder if Mr. Thurber was the bad situation my mother talked about, or if he was the one trying to save her from it. And how they can talk about all this and no one even mentions Phoebe. I don't want to look at her now. She knows, somehow, though she's so small and wouldn't understand the words, and I hate them all for her. How selfish grown-ups can be! How careless. How they so often leave it all up to us.

Layla grabs at my hand and pulls me up. Her face is wet – all our faces are wet and salted, as though we've been sprayed by a crashing wave. She is looking at me fiercely; Paul is curled up in her lap, his mouth a tight slurp around his thumb. Phoebe's gaze is set on the man in the water.

I follow her eyes and shout over the wind: "Yes, the lifeboats are ready. What shall we do, Captain?"

HONEY MAIDEN

It is somewhere deep in the thick green and yellow part of Ontario where we stop for honey. The little farm store is tidily stacked with jars in varying shades of amber and blond. There is a window white with noon sun and the honey absorbs the light, slowing it and thickening it into something that can be caught in a glass vessel. It is a moment in sepia – that golden brown, overexposed light that belongs to rural Ontario in August, belongs to honey and wheat and corn.

A woman's voice calls from a back room to tell us she'll be with us soon. Her voice, in my ear, is also thick with light. My husband, David, and I wait, turning the jars over in our hands, gazing into the centre of their goldenness, mesmerized. We finger and stroke the smooth tapered candles, the sweet smell of wax lulling us into an agrarian fantasy.

I can tell that David is imagining us as beekeepers, with netted headdresses and sturdy, canvas suits. We have been roaming the countryside looking for a place – a farm, a town, a curvature of land – to draw us in, let us settle. And while I've jabbered about almost every patch of farmers' fields we've glided past, David has been silent, even sullen, up to this point. This is my Ontario, not his. The part where there is only cornfield, occasionally spliced by towns that consist of nothing more than two dirt roads passing through each other for a brief moment.

A woman comes out from the back room, the fully-expected farm girl in the flesh, complete with cheeks fuzzed and pert as peaches, brown eyes that seem to snap. She wears cut-off jean shorts hemmed with tidy straightness, and a man's faded dress shirt, rolled to the elbows. A pin at the pocket boasts: Verna County Fair: Gold Medal Honey 1991 – last year. Attractive in an unembellished way, she is about my age.

"What can I do for yous now?" she asks in the local vernacular, but without the local twang. In fact, her words seem precise, as though she has worked to clip the curved edges from them.

David looks at her. "Do you own this farm?" His tone has an accusatory edge.

She blinks. "With my partner, yes."

"It's pretty."

She stares straight at him and I know what she means by it – only city people would call a farm pretty. "Would you like to buy some honey?"

David moistens his lips. "Do you just raise bees? I mean, not *just*, like *only*, but I mean – what I mean is, do you also grow—" He glances at me, somewhat helplessly, and I return a bemused look. "Vegetables?" He looks to me again, growing agitated. "Vegetation," he miscorrects himself. "Or – do you raise livestock?"

The woman looks at me, her mouth a straight line, her eyes sparking in a measured way. "Just bees."

David nods, his forehead pinched. He goes outside.

I lean forward and set a jar of creamed honey on the table beside a tin lunch box with compartments for quarters and loonies.

"My husband is new to farm country," I say, but the words *farm country* are awkward in my mouth. "We're newly married," I add, trying a different tact. And also, I still get a thrill saying it, though it's been a year now. "I guess you could say in the honeymoon phase, really. Or it feels that way to me."

Her eyes rest on me for a moment. "Six-fifty," she says.

Back in the car, David slides into the passenger seat and fumbles for the road map.

"Where are we?" he asks, more to himself than to me. His tone sounds so reverent I almost laugh.

"Taken with it?"

His finger moves along backroads and streams until he finds the intersection of roads we are on. For some reason, watching him, I see the map not as topographical but as anatomical. As if he is moving his finger along the curving veins of a human body. Verna. He says the word aloud. That is where we are.

Now he is unscrewing the lid off the jar. He plunges a finger in. A finger that I know from two years of holding his hand is full of tension yet creamy soft, aside from the pad with its bulbous callous from several years of adequate guitar playing.

When the honey reaches his mouth he closes his eyes and grunts. "Oh God, Sally. It's unearthly."

At that moment, and just as I am about to pull out of the laneway, there is a knucklebone tap at my window. The woman's serious, radiant face appears beside me.

"Did I forget my wallet?" I ask automatically, rolling down the window.

She looks at me as though I'm stupid. "No. It's honey in the comb. It's best that way. We give out samples." She thrusts a baby-food jar at me and then turns neatly. David swivels in his seat so fast, the seatbelt rubs hotly at his neck and his hand flies up to soothe it.

"What?" he says, turning to face me, still massaging his neck.

I hand him the jar and pull onto the road.

That evening we pitch our tent in a campground not far from the Verna honey farm. We do this wordlessly, effortlessly, the metal tubes of the tent poles fastened end to end, the swish of waterproof polyester and the satisfying clicks of plastic hooks attaching to poles, until, like magic, home appears. Afterwards, David perches on the camp chair by our weak fire with his guitar leaning against his legs, while I turn the pages of a book in the domed light of the tent.

"You're not playing," I call out after a moment. I realize that I'm not able to fully relax until I hear him pick determinedly at the strings, as he does each night at this time. There are these little rituals in marriage, I think to myself. And you don't realize how they've come to encapsulate you so soothingly, until they unravel. "Aren't you going to play?"

When he doesn't answer, I inchworm toward the window, encased in my sleeping bag, and peer out. The orange-blue of the fire casts David in black. Behind him the sky is navy blue bled through with black making David's dark form appear as part of the landscape. It is this I love about camping, the reminder of how inconsequential and yet still present humans are, but also the possibility of blending better than we do.

I have fantasies about how things could be. These are futuristic scenes that flash into mind. I think we will return to horses, for example. Well, there won't be cars, that's for sure. Let's say in 50 years, 2042, after Peak Oil, we'll be back to horses. I'd be 73 then; I hope I get to see it.

I think cities will break down – there are no models for cities to run off oil, and eventually, we will run out. But small farms, they don't necessarily require fossil fuels; we know this from the past. They can function adequately on solar and animal power. But we will need to become more humane to achieve this – more attuned to the land and to other living species.

"Do you think we could raise bees?"

David's voice is silvery through the darkness. It sounds different. A lighter tone to it. I unzip the tent and shuffle to him, settle on the grass still cocooned in my sleeping bag.

"Yes, I think we could."

He turns to me, looking startled. "Do you know anything about it, Sal?"

I look up at the sky, place the Plough. There is a trick my mom taught me, about folding your hands into a box, holding the box up to the sky, connecting the stars to the corners, shifting your hand clockwise, and there: the Little Plough, the North Star.

"A little. It's not all romantic. You've got to be careful, David."

He blinks at me, his face softening. "I will."

"Five per cent of people are deathly allergic to bee stings. It goes up 25 per cent for beekeepers."

"I've never been stung," David says, and there's a featherweight smugness to his voice. "At least not that I've noticed. I think they're not attracted to me."

"Well, that's not how it works. They sting out of defence or as a chemical response – the pheromones of a dying bee prompt nearby bees to attack. It's interesting though – a bee usually dies once it stings. Their stingers are barbed and remain in your flesh, pumping out venom long after the thorax has torn away from the head." I lower my hands and tuck them into my sleeping bag. I must have read all this somewhere – these are the kinds of things that stick to my brain, like flies to flypaper.

When I finish explaining I look to see David's eyes on me with an intensity I am now accustomed to.

"Is there anything you don't know?" he asks, and though I can't see his face, I can hear it in his voice, the pride with which he says this, but also something else – it is a hungry, greedy agitation. He slides from his seat and presses his mouth hard against mine, his hands sliding down the tube of my sleeping bag.

Somewhere in the wrestle of it, the clumsy manouevre to pull him into the sleeping bag, the tangle as we try to tug our pants down, there is a brief moment of frustration: it is always this way with David. A burst of irritation – just a passing look on his face – followed by a quick release, as though the tiny catch in him can only be found through a state of annoyance or difficulty. It's so fleeting a moment, and so instantly reversed. Certainly, as we rest against each other afterwards – the meditative pulse of crickets, the pop-crack of fire, the almost-overwhelming awesomeness of the universe spread so thickly over us – I cannot bring it up.

Within a few short weeks David has found us a house to buy in Verna. It's not all that far from the honey farm, actually. We discovered this on a walk a few days after the purchase was completed and we'd hauled our few belongings into the musty rooms of the old house. We had been following a cow path that crested a slope and I saw the farm below.

"We'll have to make friends with the honey maiden," I joked. My hand was held up to my forehead. "It's maybe a 30-minute walk."

David frowned. "I didn't realize it was so close."

I took this to mean he wished we had more space from our nearest neighbour. I reached around, rubbed his back, smiling as if to say, Look at all this land. It was all ours. But then I felt false – of course it's not ours, and I know that. It's just that I also knew thinking that way would please him. I dropped my hand.

On this morning, seeing that he looks at last settled, I bring up the idea of visiting my mother in nearby Clapton. It's the town I grew up in, and for me, proximity to my mother is one of the main draws for moving back to this area and away from Toronto. David was initially opposed to this proximity – understandably. He didn't want anyone interfering in our private future. But he looks at me now over his morning tea and nods ponderously.

"I thought you might ask," he says with a sigh through his nostrils. "I've calculated the gas and mileage. Don't make any stops if you can help it." He arches a brow at me over his teacup. "I suppose there are all sorts of old friends and ex-lovers in these parts for you."

A bark of laughter escapes me. "Hardly."

He frowns and I realize he is serious. Poor David. He can be – well, there's no other way to put it – suspicious. You can hardly blame him; he had a difficult childhood.

I bend to kiss his neck as I clear my dishes from the table. "I was a virgin until you," I remind him, whispering in his ear. He grabs my hand and pulls it to his chest, then tugs it down. It's instant for me: a switch flicked that only David knows about. I slide my fingers under his belt. With a quickness and strength he has me up on the table, my legs dangling on either side of him.

"The dishes!" I say half-heartedly, and so he pushes them roughly, which makes me laugh, deep from my throat. A bowl clatters to the floor, but doesn't break. "Hurry," is what I say next, but as soon as I say that, he slows. He pulls back to grin at me, and I have to grab him with both hands, pull him into me.

The two-hour-long drive to my mother's takes me through slow rises and descents of fecund greenness. The sky above is insistently blue. Before moving here, David and I had been living in Toronto, where we met at university, and married a year later. But it already seems forgotten, our urban existence. I am wondering, as I move through the familiar landscape of rural Ontario, how I survived Toronto so long and why I didn't answer the call to leave sooner. Well, that last part I know – David felt we needed to earn a certain amount of money before leaving our respective jobs. He's eight years older than me and already had a small fortune saved up from consistent, relentless work on construction sites. I added to it once we'd decided I should quit school and started working two jobs. He handles the books for our pooled resources. At the point when we'd earned enough to put money down on some land, he gave his notice and let me know it was time I could do the same.

David had grown up in the suburbs, but spent a lot of time in Toronto. He'd been a teenager when it was discovered that his dad, a trader who commuted and also kept a condo in the city, had a second family. In the second family was a boy David's age. He doesn't like to talk about this, has only told me about it in parentheses. The funny thing is his dad is really kind of a hippie. I met him once – good with numbers and completely despicable for what he did, but also very passionate about living in an alternative way, an urban version of it.

We went for dinner at his dad's city condo, David standing behind a kitchen chair while his dad explained about a loophole for raw milk farmers – selling such milk is illegal, but anyone can obtain raw milk if they own the cow, so the farmers sell shares in the cows. He'd just bought a share in a Holstein and offered us glasses of pungent milk from a glass bottle. David began shouting at him. He was jabbing at buttons in the elevator when I caught up to him, having grabbed both our coats and thanked his dad for the milk.

"I can't stand there talking to him without thinking he's lying to me," David said. His voice cracked and a tremor took hold of his hands. He held them out, staring at them, then looked up at me. I'd never seen anyone's eyes so racked with grief. He stepped forward and collapsed onto me, delicately, his head on my shoulder. The doors closed, but neither of us pressed Lobby. We stood in the elevator like that for many minutes.

My mother's house, the home I grew up in, is what would now be called a heritage farm home. She would call that nonsense – a house is just a house, she'd say. We had a few chickens and, at one time, a cow, but that was all. My mom adopted me, raised me on her own. It was just the two of us, the dogs, the chickens, the farmhouse. Card games at the kitchen table, falling asleep beside her on the couch covered by the orange and brown afghan, early morning walks out to the garden to pick flowers when they're pert and hold drops of dew, like diamonds in cupped hands, at their centres.

The road to her house is still dirt, and after following it a while it begins to feel like a pathway, a worn and trampled pass between rows of maples, elms, and willows. The trees bow toward each other in varying angles and postures so that driving past them, they appear like images in a flip book – a stuttering animation of trees that whirl and curtsy and lean. I have a sudden memory of seeing them this way as a child, my head leaning against Mom's arm as she drove us to and from the house in our pickup truck. The gasoline smell of it, her cotton sleeve.

It's been a difficulty for me, going this long without seeing her. I have to admit that. Two years is a long time. David didn't want anyone but us at the wedding, so not even then did I see her, although she was the first person I called on the phone afterwards. I've had to put her out of mind – which I don't like to do.

I like it even less as I get closer to the house and smell the warm earth and cow manure. I feel a sort of dissolving, as though I'd pulled something tightly around me and now it is loosening, just enough that other air can seep in. Familiar air. How is it that smells can do this to us? Rush into our bodies, permeate the skin and re-enter the blood stream, changing us from the inside out into who we used to be. I play over in my mind all David's reasons for delaying seeing her while we lived in the city: gas and mileage, savings, focus on our life together, no one else's. He was married before, to Bridget, who played guitar and had long hair to her waist, the colour of cherry wood. But Bridget's friends and family interfered too much, David said. They ruined it. Yes, we will make our own choices. Even if others don't understand.

Mom is outside sitting on the back step between pots of orange marigolds, her elbows on her knees, and her chin resting in the cup of one hand. She is drooping forward about to doze off, but then spots my car and raises one long thin arm and flaps it around. "Sally! Sally!" as though I might miss her and drive past.

"I'm so glad you could make it around to see me," she says after a long, firm embrace. We walk into the kitchen. I smile – that's unemotional country talk; we're both much more than glad. The screen door whaps shut behind us. An achingly familiar smell – cut flowers and coffee – rushes to meet me. The house looks as though it has sunken into itself since I was last here.

"Are you doing all right?" We ask each other at the same time with the same inflection, and then laugh. She holds her elbows in her hands and leans back as she laughs. I see the gold fillings in her molars. Her hair is cropped extra short and is now so fine I can see her tanned scalp through it.

"This is nice," I say, rubbing my palm across her head.

She reaches up and holds my hand there. "Much cooler."

"David says hello."

Mom nods. "Well. That's good of him. And where is David now?"

I pluck a peach from the basket on the table, hold it to my nose, then smile at her. "We found a place, Mom. Not too far, actually. In Verna."

Mom makes a little gasp and her fingers fly up to her mouth. "Oh! I'm so pleased." She pulls me in for a squeeze and then steps back, still holding me by the arms. Her grip is strong for a woman who looks so thin and aged. "Does this mean I'll be able to see you more?"

"Mom, I can see you whenever you like. Whenever I like."

She looks at me steadily for a moment. Her eyes are pale green, like sea glass. There's a fine layer of water on them always. I think it has come with age.

I notice the water accumulating before she blinks. "Well, I hope that it's true," she says. "I hope we can see each other just as much as we like."

After we eat peaches, drink coffee, and talk, I climb the stairs to my old bedroom. Mom has left it more or less the same. Plain and clean. Full of books. There is an old radio on the desk with its innards exposed – I used to like taking machines apart and creating new ones from their delicate cogs and wires, like knuckles and veins. I dimly recall sitting there, five years ago, playing inventor. The window is open wide, and the bed looks freshly made. There is a glass and a carafe of water on the bedside table as well as a tubular vase with a single day lily picked at just the right moment, as only Mom can do, its wing-like petals having just burst from the pod.

"Oh, Mom," I turn to her, suddenly realizing. "I'm not spending the night. I need to get back to David, and the house."

She pauses, having just come up the steps behind me. One long, flat hand is resting on the wall, and I can see she requires this slight brace. "Oh, that's all right. I was just hoping."

Something on the wall catches my eye and I step forward. "You framed it."

"Mmm," Mom says. "It should be commemorated. That golden moment."

The letter behind glass catches the light so that it seems like something polished and stone, as if the embossed words are carved into marble. I feel the same thrill as I first felt six years ago, at age 17, pulling it from the envelope and reading it in my hands at the end of our laneway. *Dear Ms. Sally Maribel Dryden, We are pleased to inform you that you are the recipient of the 1986 Rural Academic Achievement Scholarship.*

This is how I went to York University on a full scholarship with everything paid for – tuition, books, housing, even a meal card. We could never have afforded university otherwise.

The competition had been fierce for the scholarship. Everyone in the rural parts of the province who wanted to go to school volunteered at all the right places, studied exhaustively, and worked hell-bent on their projects. I had created a miniature world – Future Farm, I called it – in which a minute series of solar panels and tiny wind turbines generated actual electricity so that the lights of the small farmhouse – a clean, modern structure – glowed.

All competitors from my own and surrounding counties had gathered at a community centre to set up their projects. A team of adjudicators walked down the rows frowning at our hard work. The house and turbine of Future Farm were set into living soil. I had found a variety of grass that grew in tiny scope, planted several bonsai trees which I kept trimmed, fashioned a simple irrigation system from copper tubing as slender as a flower's stem.

I can still remember the face of one of those adjudicators as she leaned over my tiny farm, her gleaming black bob sliding forward as she brought her face close to the farmhouse window, impassioned scribbling on her clipboard. She paused, her face a hard knot behind her glasses. Later, she handed me back my application form with her comments scrawled along the bottom: *An extraordinary capacity to actualize her vision.*

But university felt overwhelming. The city was cacophonous and it stank. I could not seem to find a space quiet enough to sort my own mental workings; my thoughts came out both ruptured and askew. I became unpopular – perhaps I came off as a little oracular. I drifted through the city, feeling as though the streets had been sewn together haphazardly by some madcap inventor; no pacifying, clarifying logic or intelligence at play.

It was during this lonely season that I met David.

A few mornings after visiting Mom, I sleep in and wake to find I'm alone in bed. There's a note beside the kettle: Gone for supplies. He's full steam ahead on the beekeeping idea. At night he leaves the lamp on beside me in our new bedroom, his finger running underneath the words of an apiculture guide. During the day he's often out, gathering what he needs – a smoker and a hooked tool he calls a *queen excluder scraper*. But that's his way. He catches wind of an idea and becomes obsessive about it.

Of course, that's how he had come to the decision to leave the city. He'd taken to my vision of sustainable small farms surpassing the age of cities. The enthusiasm with which I relayed my ideas, while repelling everyone else, seemed to draw him in. He began to say we could build a farm, much like Future Farm, and live off-grid. After a while, it was all he talked about.

Yet, now that we are here, now that we have bought the house and a small square of land, he seems preoccupied. Yesterday, I laced up my shoes in the morning and turned to him: "I'm going to walk the perimeter of our property, see if I can visualize where different crops might best thrive. Want to come?"

He was standing at the counter, two jars of honey in front of him. He dipped a spoon into one, licked it clean, then the other, his face folded in concentration. "Can't you do that on your own?" he'd asked.

This morning, I eat toast and then decide to walk to the Verna honey farm. I'd like to buy a pillar candle for the next time I visit my mother, as well as a jar of honeycomb. I walk along the old cow path through purple clover and when I get there, the farm feels quiet, perhaps unawake. There is no one in the farm store, but no matter. I recall the system of honesty boxes in these parts. Farmers leaving their plums and zucchini out in baskets on card tables with a shoebox left to collect coins.

I am standing in the small farm store when I hear a screen door slam, probably up at the house, hurried footsteps in the gravel outside, a shout, and then a cry. I move to the window. The woman from before is rushing across the farmyard toward me, a look of fury on her face. I look behind her and to the sides of her – I thought the cry I'd heard sounded like a man's – but I see no one else.

She bursts through the door and halts when she sees me. "Oh!" Her fingers go up and comb through her hair hastily. "What are you doing here?" she asks, her voice rough.

"I'm sorry," I say without thinking. "I can come another time. I was just stopping for this candle. And some honey."

She glances out the window and her eyes flick back to mine. "Look—" she starts, her voice angry. She breathes through her nose in an agitated way. "You're – you're—"

"Um." I glance at the door. "I'll just come another time."

She watches me, but still says nothing for a moment. Then: "It's six-fifty. For the jar. The candles are ten."

"Oh. All right." I reach into my back pocket and then feel a swerve in my stomach. "Oh no. I'm sorry." Now I feel extra ridiculous. Obviously, she's in the middle of some personal crisis and I've made her come down here and she didn't want to and now I can't even pay. "I must have forgotten my wallet. I thought I had…"

"You don't remember me, do you?"

I look up from my hands. The brown eyes glitter.

"I'm sorry," I say, feeling like a fool for apologizing to her three times in the past 30 seconds and having no idea what for.

"You're Sally Dryden," she says. "You won the Rural Achievement scholarship back in '86."

I blink at her.

"I wouldn't be so surprised," she says, her voice serrated at the edges. "You were a local celebrity all that summer. Your name on all the shop windows. I remember your project. It was ridiculous."

She looks at me expectantly, but I swallow back another "I'm sorry."

"I almost went through a nervous breakdown pulling my application together. My parents kept telling me to not put so much stock in it. They just wanted me to get married and farm." She looks me up and down as she says this. "I'm a smart person." She steps closer to me. "They wouldn't give me any money for education. Not a dollar. We made a deal. They said, if you win this scholarship, you can go. If you don't, you stay. No more talk of school."

We stand, our eyes at the exact same level. I feel all my breath balled in my throat.

"I was going to be a neurosurgeon," she says and her fingers rise in the air like smoke. "I like the mechanics of our brains. And I have very calm hands." She looks at her hands for a moment, and I look at her looking at them. "Ironically, this does seem to serve me as a beekeeper."

When her eyes flash toward mine, I turn my gaze quickly to her hands, so perfectly still in the air. She has remarkably long fingers with nails that look as though they've been rounded with mathematical precision; fingers that indeed look like they could cut and sew into the minute tunnels of our brains.

"I'm so sorry," I say and this time I know what for.

"Well. I'm sure you've already graduated, with honours no doubt, and are on to grad school by this point." When I don't respond right away, her eyes pull back to me.

I blink at her, stupidly, and she frowns.

"Aren't you?"

I know that I should just nod, but I can't for some reason, and then I hear myself say: "Well, I didn't – I didn't actually graduate."

She jerks her head.

"I left just before graduating." I moisten my lips. Why am I telling her this? "I hated university," I go on. "All those people there to party and read the same ideas without really turning them over while the world around is changing rapidly. Here we are on the brink of environmental crisis, the solution literally at our feet, and nobody cares. None of them thought far enough. I felt like I didn't belong there. Until I met David." I grin at her, but she does not return the smile and I attach my gaze to the floor. "He made me feel like I was smart again," I say. I'm surprised to hear it come out like I have to prove something to her. "He really supported me. He helped me understand that I was – well, that I was above all that, as he said. The institution of education, I mean. I mean, that's what he called it and that's what he said. It sounds a little arrogant saying it now, actually, but I don't think he means it that way. So I dropped out and got a job and saved up, and then we came here." I am still looking at the floor, but I peek upward and then have to look back down again, the expression on her face is so violent.

"You dropped out," she says, her voice tamped.

I lift my head. "Yes, I—"

"Dropped out. And what? Forfeited the money?" Her voice is still quiet, but her eyes flicker at me. "For that asshole?"

"Hey!" I frown. "My husband is not an asshole."

"Your *husband*," she says, for some reason making air quotes around the word, and now her voice is no longer quite so contained, "has been coming around here the past few weeks sniffing at me like a dog and came here today and – and tried to have sex with me!"

I balk at her and it takes me a moment to find my voice. When I do I can hear myself in a strange way – like I am next to myself, hearing my voice. "What did you say? Did he—" The words cling to my throat. "Did he *seduce* you?"

"God!" Her hands fly up to her face and cover it. "No. He tried to. Badly." I catch a sliver of eye between her fingers. "He didn't know what he was dealing with."

I stare at her, my brain stuck against my skull. "I don't understand this. I'm not – I'm sorry – why didn't you tell me when I first came in?" The words are like melting wax in my mouth.

She drops her hands and makes a sour face. "As in, *'Good morning, that'll be ten dollars, and by the by, your husband's been trying to fuck me?'*" She looks at me for a moment and then sighs and says, in a somewhat less angry voice: "He was just leaving when you got here. He went out by the front door when you came in by the back. Maybe you can catch him. If you want."

Her last few words hang strangely in the air. If I want. The word *want* is like an insect flying insistently toward the light of my mind. It keeps fluttering into me. I find myself trying to remember what it is that I want. David doesn't necessarily ask. My Future Farm, really. To scoop the living soil of these farmlands into my palms and press my nose in it. To use my brain to change the course of things.

At that moment we hear yelling. A woman's voice coming from the direction of the farmhouse saying, "Muriel! That guy! He's been stung!"

We look at each other, then run out the door. A tall, black woman with curls is sprinting toward us, a cordless phone held up to her ear. "I just got home to our farm," she yelps into the phone, while waving us frantically around the side of the house toward a supine shape at the base of an elm tree. Beside the tree is a stack of beehives around which a silvery haze of bees undulates, zinging in threatening tones. "A man has been stung repeatedly by our bees! I've just found him. I think he's suffered anaphylactic shock." She gives the address and hangs up the phone and shouts: "We don't have an EpiPen, Muriel!"

Muriel and I meet eyes. She does not look nearly as panicked as the black woman. Muriel, instead, looks sharp, vivid. She is alert to all details, I can see that. It is almost like watching her read the situation. I wait for her to jump forward, apply some kind of immediate medical help, but then I notice that I am waiting, still. She stands perfectly immobilized, focused and primed for action, but taking none. I understand this as diagnostic inaction; I pull my eyes from her and step forward.

I find the pitch of the bees and I begin to hum like them and then I hum more quietly than them. I pretend it is the future and we can blend with our environments. I imagine they might understand me, in some way of their own, at least understand that I am not trying to hurt them, that I just need to get to the human amidst them; and I begin to move through the bees, raising my hands and moving them slowly back and forth as though walking through water. Inside the tunnel of bees, I kneel slowly at David's side. His face is unevenly puffed, like a marshmallow cooked at a campfire. His lips grey-blue. I'm aware of the women saying things to me, shouting, but I can't make defined words of the sounds. For a brief flash, I muse that perhaps I am a kind of bee myself. All my actions seem to come in response to the pheromones in the air around me. My hands seem to move without me, tilting David's head back by the forehead, pinching his nose, sealing his mouth with my dry lips. One puff, two puffs. Push-push-push-push-push on the chest. Again and again with the bees around me and their voices blending until it is all one droning sound and the elm tree and David's body and then there is the smell of smoke, hands on my shoulders, human voices becoming clearer, a paramedic with his sleeves rolled up, arms thick with hair, a needle jammed into David's thigh right through his pants, a gurney that clatters like a grocery cart, the back doors of the ambulance clipping shut, a silence. A silence which fills in a rush with the sound of two women speaking to me at the same time.

"Sit."

"Put your feet up. Like this."

"We should have had an EpiPen, Muriel."

"Don't talk about that now, Julie."

"We can take you to the hospital."

"Drink a little water."

"We'll take you. Come on."

Somehow I fall asleep, maybe slide unconscious is a better way of putting it, on the 45-minute drive to the hospital some distance behind the ambulance. I wake when the truck engine cuts and when I open my eyes, I see through the haze of my half-conscious state, Muriel and the other woman, Julie, with their arms around each other, Muriel's nose tucked into Julie's neck. Muriel notices me and jolts. "I'll walk you to the door," she says.

We walk across the hospital parking lot. I feel confused, as though I had been asleep for days, not just minutes. I know David is through the glass doors, in a room.

"Please don't tell anyone," Muriel says, her voice cutting through the cotton thickness around me.

I look at her for a long moment, allow her face to come into focus. Her brown eyes are like molasses slowly pouring from a pitcher. I clear my throat. "Which part?" I ask, genuinely unsure.

Now she looks perturbed and the eyes flash. "The Julie part. No one really knows."

"Oh." I glance back at the truck. Of course. Small towns.

I cannot find my voice, though I have a sudden urge to tell her that the only thing that should matter in a relationship is that the right things are caught tightly. And nothing else. Catch nothing else tightly. Instead I nod, to show her I care, to show her I give my available concern to her.

She dips her head at me. It is the first real gesture of softness I've seen from her. "And what will you do now, Sally?"

What will I do?

It's as though some part of me breaks through a skin, standing there in the parking lot: "Leave him." I clear my throat. "I'm going to leave him."

Muriel's eyes turn a deep and sudden shade of black. "Oh, Sally," she says, shaking her head. "Sally, I don't think he's going to make it."

"I know," I say. I feel like everything is moving in slow motion as I raise one hand and in response she raises one of hers, and then I turn and walk toward the glass doors.

The weather turned a few weeks later. The house sold quickly. All the money – a heavy stack of bills – came to me, of course. The money from the house, plus all of David's, which actually was partly mine anyway. I could pay to finish my degree now – and pay for another one if I wanted to.

On the morning I leave the house, the sun comes up a pink-orange lozenge. It makes the hills, the fields, the trees turn caramel. I have the sudden, distinct impression that if I could press down on this landscape with a giant fork, the layers of earth would look like honeycomb and from those hexagons, golden honey would ooze out. It is a sweet, warm land. I pass a field planted with solar panels; their black, glinting faces turned toward the dawn like sunflowers. I turn the car into the lane for Verna honey. It is too early for anyone to be awake and in the store, I know that, but I want that candle for my mother, and some honeycomb too. I don't want to see Muriel again anyway. But there will be an honesty box.

I leave there lighter.

As I drive past the yellow fields I allow myself just one brief moment of fantasizing: Muriel in a bright room, a delicate hooked tool in her precise fingers. She slips the sharp blade into the wires of her patient's gleaming brain. The coiled tubing opens its miniature contents to her, the way a pod releases a cluster of petals.

HOUSE CALLS

It happens that Thursday that I am walking home from my office along the back road and I see, coming from somewhere on Anthony's farm, a a soft mushroom of smoke bloom in the air. It might be a bonfire, burning up brush, but I decide to cut through Anthony's field to be sure. I'll suss it out and if I need to alert him, I will. Otherwise, I'll keep on walking, I think to myself.

I follow the familiar, beaten-down footpath through the gap in the fence posts Anthony left open for me years ago. I notice the cornfields are only half ploughed – late for October. A tractor that has been left at the edge of the field has its two front tires halfway sunk into the muck. It makes me think of a lame horse, struggling to get to its feet. The closer I get to passing the sunbleached stone farmhouse, the more I feel an urge to knock on the door.

It has been long enough, I think.

Anthony's mother, Tabitha, comes to the door. "Oh! Dr. Olshefsky!"

"Just Anna," I say, not for the first time. "Is Anthony—"

"We're having dinner." She looks behind her, and then back to me, her face a starched smile.

From behind her there comes a swooshing sound and a thump, and Tabitha crouches. "Jayla, you're a mess!" She says it with a tremble of laughter. A small head covered in knotted-up dirty blonde fluff peeps around the corner.

"Dr. Oshuff," the girl says. She has a fierce smudge of dirt across her upper lip, as though she's been eating soil by the spoonful.

I crouch down, too. "Hello, Jayla. My, it's good to see you." I branch out my arms and she shuffles in, rooting into me and smelling a bit like smoke. As I take another sniff, Tabitha swoops down and scoops her up.

"I'm hungry now, Oma."

Tabitha looks at me, still starchy. "Well, we're *about* to have dinner."

"I was walking by and noticed smoke," I say.

She looks at me strangely. "And?"

I am not sure what her expression is trying to tell me – she seems almost annoyed.

"Just being a good neighbour," I say.

Tabitha pauses. "Well, it's all under control if that's what you're wondering."

"Well then. Is Anthony here?"

Tabitha stiffens her arms around the little girl, but Jayla throws her head back and whelps, "Daddy!" then wriggles and grunts her way down her grandmother's belly and clomps along the hallway. "I'll get him, Dr. Oshuff!"

Tabitha watches her disappear around a corner, then turns back to me. She has on a pilly woollen outfit that makes her look like a pair of socks, rolled together into a tube. She's clinically obese; it's been a struggle for her. Last time I saw her she'd been down 60 pounds on a medical diet, but it looks like all progress has been lost. That must have been months ago – more? I'd been in my office, looking down, and spotted her, talking with someone, her body collapsing to the side as it does when she laughs. I asked for that office on the upper floor. The things you learn about your patients just by having a second-floor window.

There's a thick quietness between us on the porch now. I wait politely for Tabitha to ask me in.

"Well," she says, "how's the practice?"

"Oh, just fine. Flu season, you know. How's everyone here?"

"Everyone is fine. Really."

"Stephanie?" That's Jayla's mother, Anthony's girlfriend.

"Everyone," Tabitha says. She gives me a weary, though firm look.

I reach out to touch her on the arm. "This is not a house call," I say, gently.

Tabitha releases a puff of air, and sags, then shakes her head at me. "It wasn't last time, either." She clears her throat. "Everything is going so well, Anna, I promise. I look after Jayla most days. Stephanie got a job at Kitty's Kitchen in town – regular work. Anthony's very busy with the farm. Hell of a lot of work to bring it back. We haven't sown the fields for years. Well, you know all that." She looks at me so steadily I have to remind myself that *I* am the doctor. Really, I think to myself, if anyone's examining anyone. "He's not doing anything he's not supposed to," Tabitha adds.

"And what *is* he doing?" I ask, but before she can answer we are intercepted.

"Dr. Olshefsky?" It's Stephanie, appearing at the top of the stairs.

Stephanie is a girl who thinks more is more when it comes to makeup – though it's usually skillfully applied. Today, she has a smudge below one eye and her hair is as tangled as her daughter's. She seems pale, too, an almost bluish white, and reedier than usual. She looks at her mother-in-law, then back at me.

"Just a social call," Tabitha says to her. "She saw the smoke. And now she wants to say hi to Anthony. Jayla's gone to get him, but maybe he's too busy right now?" She turns so that her face is away from mine, and so I glance up at Stephanie, to read her face as it reads her mother-in-law's. Some of my patients, you've got to be able to read them in a flash. So much they don't say to the doctor.

Up at the top of the stairs, Stephanie shrugs. "Probably," she says. She comes down the steps, quickly. Like a pony, I think, her skinny legs skittish and light.

It isn't a secret that I never really warmed to Stephanie. But then, Anthony and I had been best friends a long time before she came to town and introduced him to some bad habits. Right about the time I graduated from medical school and came back to our rural hospital to practice, she'd gotten pregnant. There were a number of men who could have been the father, but she seemed sure it was Anthony. Because I am one of a handful of doctors in town, I know he never really pressed the point.

Stephanie stops when she is a few inches from my face, her breath smelling brightly of Listerine. "Maybe another time, Anna." It seems to me she sways a bit. I think briefly of a tower made from playing cards. Anthony and I used to construct them, sitting on the kitchen floor, in the room there, past Tabitha and down the hallway. One puff of breath and down they fall.

When we were little, Anthony and I walked home from school together and Tabitha put out snacks for us. Little Debbies or Joe Louies. I was never allowed junk food in my house and it was a wonder to me, those strange and heavy lumps in your hand, the cellophane puckered around them, the thickness in your throat. My mother called Tabitha one time and, to my embarrassment, asked that she not give me any more snacks as I was refusing dinner once I got home. This was a lie; I ate my mother's roasted chickens and wholewheat buns and buttered spinach. And Tabitha knew it was a lie, too. She started giving us baby carrots – those tasteless, wooden things – and "lite" ranch dressing from a plastic squeeze bottle, and acting nervous around my mother. Truth to be told, though, a lot of people found it difficult to be easy around my mother. She was ahead of her time for this small town – she was the one who managed the family store and insisted I go to university. "Poor Tabitha," she'd say. "Forced into nursing her husband because he was forced into the factory."

Most people in town work on the assembly lines at The Foundry. Lord knows I've treated my share of sliced hands. But for Anthony's family, it was a particularly raw deal. Anthony's father loved to farm, would've farmed until he fell over dead in the field if he could have. Not many of them do. They farm because it's all they know, most of them. Except Anthony's father – there was a pride in it for him. A feeling that he was in tune with his crops, could read their growth and decay. But the money never came, he went to The Foundry, started drinking, and Tabitha had to quit her job as nurse, just to keep it all together. This was when Anthony and I were teenagers.

Just at that moment, Anthony comes trudging around the side of the house and halts at the bottom of the porch steps when he sees me.

He looks brown and broad. Always been strong as a working horse. Or almost always. Jayla is perched on his shoulders, tapping his head. I try to get a good read of his face – I could do it in a fraction of a glance, I know him so well – but have just made eye contact when he reaches up to swing Jayla up and over, loop-de-loop, to land on her feet with a squeal.

"Pretty busy today, Anna," Anthony says and squints, looking away. Jayla tugs at his hand and his mouth twitches into that barely-there grin of his. He loves her so much. I've no doubt of that. That's partly why I keep an eye out. Just to be sure everything is all right. He'd never forgive himself for losing track of how much he loves her, the way his dad did with him.

"Can we show Dr. Oshuff the project?" Jayla asks, her face turned all the way up to his, her head back so she can see him way up there. I follow her gaze, picture Anthony and I walking along the edge of the cornfield, Jayla on his shoulders.

"No." Then he says nothing, and I shake my head quickly.

"That's all right. I really—" I have to stop and cough. My throat feels dry suddenly and this annoys me. A rasp of smoke. There are a thousand things I am used to saying into these particular gaps. How many times has a patient glared softly at me from his chair when I ask a benign-enough question. It's just one of those things – people feel awkward around doctors. Especially small-town people. But standing here now, for some reason, I cannot think of anything to pour into the crag between us. I cough again and I hear the tiniest sigh from Anthony. I know what he means by it: impatience. And now I'm wasting his time. A strange wash of embarrassment comes over me; I brace against it. I've only ever acted according to my conscience and my profession.

It's a funny thing about becoming a doctor in your small, rural hometown. All of a sudden you know the people you've always known much more intimately – and those you already knew intimately, you see as though through a microscope. You see their rashes, ear infections, and back acne. You see their varicose veins and sometimes you see other things – tiny bird tracks up and down their brown forearms.

"Jayla, come inside with me. We'll get some dinner started." Stephanie's eyes are on Anthony. She holds out a hand and Jayla bounds to her.

And sometimes you drop in, as you've done hundreds of times since childhood, to say hi to your friend, and his pregnant girlfriend, and see too many empty liquor bottles.

And if you're a doctor, what do you do?

I think about the last time I was here, pushing my way upstairs, finding Stephanie in bed.

She just didn't know any better, I came to think. Everything I told her about being pregnant seemed genuinely new to her. So I am glad that I talked to her, that I made her come in every week during the pregnancy to educate her, keep an eye on her. The healthier she got, the more embarrassed she became. But it all came out all right in the end; Jayla is proof of that. And there wasn't a friendship to lose with Stephanie anyhow.

"Hot dogs?" Jayla asks.

"No!" Stephanie shoots a look at me. "Vegetable soup and buns. I can cook now," she says, and it is clear she is directing the last piece of information at me.

I nod. "I hear you're working at the diner."

"Yes. And not just waiting tables – line cook," she straightens up. "I'm tired as hell – getting over a bad flu – but it's good money. And I like it."

I can see it then. The mark of a flu having passed through her small body. "Drink lots of fluids," I tell her. "Water's the best."

"That's all I drink lots of now," she says, and there is something in her voice – she gives me a small smile. The smile is new to me; I suddenly see something in her face I haven't noticed before – a quality of softness or pure, unforced gratitude, and it throws me. She appears almost wholesome with her face this way.

"Jayla's growing like a weed," I say, meaning to extend something back to her, and Stephanie nods eagerly.

"Well, goodbye, Anna," she says. She stands with her hands on Jayla's shoulders and looks down at her. "Come on, munchkin." Jayla throws her head back and makes a funny face – eyes partially crossed and teeth bared. I laugh, but I'm the only one. They wave goodbye and go back inside and Tabitha moves to join them, but I am not quite able to step away. I am trying to examine Anthony out of the corner of one eye, but he keeps shifting his body away, digging his toe at the ground.

When we were teenagers, Anthony and I carved out a secret room for ourselves in the barn loft. When his father had been sober he was curt, sewn up. Beer had made him sloppy and awkward, so then he would disappear to be drunk alone, to nurse his embarrassment at the slightly-off things he would blurt out in a too-loud voice. I see it in the hospital now and then – factory men who put the work on, like a costume, and slowly lose themselves in the folds. Sometimes they drink to forget it's just a job. There's no pride in it, but there is a certain security in having a station in life. Any station. That's what my mother called it: "Don't settle for a low station," she'd say. It seemed like a secret; something no other parent said to their child in this town. But a secret I always thought Anthony was in on.

"What's the project?" I ask now, standing on the porch.

Tabitha's hands flutter up and then settle over her soft belly. "Nothing," she says.

"We're building an in-law suite for Mom," Anthony says. "She's going to live on the property, but in her own place. A one-floor deal."

Tabitha sighs. "It's my joints. I've gained back all the weight and then some." She shakes her head, sucking in her lips. "It's shameful," she says, almost so quietly I don't hear. "Imagine having to have a special house built for you."

"It's nothing to be embarrassed about," Anthony says.

"Of course it isn't," I say quickly – too quickly, it seems. Anthony looks at me for the first time and now I am the one who has to look away.

I can feel him studying me and as long as his gaze is on me, my face feels sunburnt, stinging-nettle hot. I think about all the years Anthony was my best friend, all the afternoons spent here on this farm, walking along the tractor trails, talking about, well, life, I guess you'd call it. His itch to see Spain and mine to see New Zealand, the injustices of the world, the infamous seventh-grade field trip to Quebec City during which we rode side by side, there and back, in our own tiny world the size of a bus seat. I look out across the farm now and *see* these conversations, like moths, sheer and fleeting. So thick I'd have to brush them away from my face if I stepped off the porch and into the field. It all feels so unfinished to me. I want to turn to him now and say, "I went to New Zealand. You know that. I know that you know that. So why don't you ever ask me about it?" I know, too, he never got to Spain.

Suddenly he turns his eyes to the direction of the smoke. "I better get back to it. We're burning up the brush. We need the space for Mom's new place."

Something in me leaps up. My throat feels hot and tight. It's as though I both want to speak and don't know how to speak anymore. If there was a way to tell him that we doctors wear costumes, too. But why should that keep us from what is all around us here in these fields? Our past conversations and exchanges so real I can smell them. Here, lying fallow. I swallow at the rocks in my throat.

But Anthony speaks before I can. "You've done enough, Dr. Olshefsky. We don't need anyone checking in on us." And then he turns and walks away, and I watch for as long as I can, just wanting to grip him in my sight. When I finally look away, I recall that I am standing there with Tabitha, who folds her arms across her belly awkwardly and looks at me with that odd expression on her face.

Finally, she sighs: "Honestly, Anna, you think we wouldn't be aware of smoke on our own farm?" she says, before going inside and closing the door quietly behind her.

My face becomes warmer with the soft thunk of the door closing.

I blink at the closed door and feel my eyes sweep over it, as though trying to read something there. I will turn and go; I will.

But for a brief moment, I close my eyes and allow myself to imagine that Tabitha stepped aside and swept me in and I am sitting at the table with Jayla while Stephanie ladles out soup and they all tell me about something funny or smart Jayla did last week. And Anthony will come in from the fields and he will turn and look at me the way he used to look at me, with the smells of the farm around us, in our plain clothes and faces.

EQUIPOISE

Alex's form was one that took time to notice. It was many years before I could see it myself. Perhaps this is because he began as my husband's friend and my husband never spoke of it. And because when we qualify a person as belonging to someone else, and not our own, we only look so closely. In fact, I've come to think how we qualify anything is how we know how closely to look.

Alex and his wife, Ren, and my husband, Brian, and I have all known each other for many years. It's 14 years for me now, out here on the West Coast. We have children and houses and lives that spill into each other's and sometimes become mixed and interchangeable. Aside from the camping trips and potluck evenings spent drinking beer and talking around the kitchen table, there have been other, more substantial overlaps. I have rushed to the side of the road to kneel by Alex's dog after she was hit by a Canada Post truck. His children are often in my care, either directly or peripherally. Other than Alex, I am the only one who knows how to disengage their unruly furnace. I am intimate, in other words, with this man's life. I hold the truth of that responsibility in a firm hand, and yet, year in year out, I never saw it.

Then today, this morning, I was sitting in the kitchen, nursing Max and looking out the rounded window that juts out over our front lawn and caught sight of him, careening around the corner on his bicycle. He was leaning gently into the curve and gliding. So seamless was this action – the slight bend of the cul-de-sac, the diagonal streaks of lemony morning light, the tilt of the bicycle, and his body's weight dipping softly toward the moist, sponge-like pavement – that the lines of it were echoed everywhere. I suddenly saw the way the power lines could be seen as artistically arranged, leading the eye up and to the right, straight into the pinkest, most luminous part of the sky. A mass of swallows rose in one perfect glob, a cursive swoosh of black ink. They settled like tinkling glass in a cherry tree whose buds were just beginning to blush more white than rose. I was suspended in the smooth, almost liquid nature of it all. The way everything definite loses its hard hold when, for just a handful of seconds, you are in the present only.

I saw him clearly, as part of the instant, his face reflecting the early light, the way his eyes gave away his constant worry and delight in the world, the familiar navy-blue sweater whose salty smell I knew, the off-kilter shoulders and pained-looking angle of the neck – and then there it was, in the cervical spine. How had I not noticed before? I had a sudden rush of compassion for this man whom I love; I had a sudden realization that I loved him. Not in any romantic sense whatsoever, but simply in a way that is available to any of us at any time to love another, simply because we are human and because we know, so well, how anguishing it can be to be human. And we also know, so well, how desperately hard we are all trying, just to provide ourselves and our children and our husbands and wives and parents with a sense of meaning, a sustained feeling of ease and joy. It was a moment of pure, unfiltered, anthropological fondness, and then Max, half-asleep, sawed his new tooth against my nipple.

My mind tilted. A new disc slid into slot and began to whir, playing out a familiar, not altogether unpleasant, tune. I had my identity back and with it the defined edges of my body, the window frame, and my preoccupations. The electrical wires regained a bland functionality and blurred into grainy background noise until I no longer noticed them. I resumed my own background hum – near to the sound my refrigerator emits – of the curiosity, and its encasing rind of the regular, garden-variety fear that I live with and have lived with and suppose I will always live with.

But this, too, is available, I thought to myself.

Alex disappeared behind the rose bush which has no roses yet, dipped out of view, then dipped back in. My eyes went directly to the unevenness of him and I realized I would, from now on, see his form – a shape like a favourite cup broken and glued back together, but improperly. I could never be blind to it again. I had a feeling of gladness, of being made tender, about this: I could see him now.

Later that same morning, after walking my two older children, the twins, to school and returning home with the third, baby Max, I answer a phone call from Alex's wife, Ren.

"Can you come be with me for a moment, Erin?" she asks. I shift Max to my stronger hip, holding the phone more firmly to my ear.

"Is everything all right?"

"I just need another adult for a minute."

I have only to walk a few steps. Out our front gate, a diagonal cut across the street, up her steps. It is early spring, the first week actually. Here in Victoria, that means mid-February. We are all – except Ren, who was born and raised here – from Ontario, and the papery, bulbous heads of crocuses, in a month I used to associate with skating lessons and head colds, still give me a moment's pause. I feel as though I have found a secret place, a parallel world, unfathomable to my Ontario self.

In fact, I am still in awe of our situation – that is, that we live in a nice home in a good neighbourhood in an absurdly pretty and grotesquely expensive city. It happened by accident for all of us – except Ren, of course. There was probably never any question anywhere along the line of her life that she would always live here. She is inextricable with this city in my mind. And in hers too, I'd wager.

My husband, Brian, and Ren's husband, Alex, were childhood best friends in Ontario, but then Alex's family moved here when he turned eleven. Years later, Brian and Alex reunited at the University of Victoria, falling easily back into their friendship as though they'd worked to maintain a taut bow between their polar existences while apart, when really, they hadn't written or phoned, not once in seven years. This gap of time and space in their life together seems unimportant, a quality I marvel at as I fear the cords that connect me to those I love back home may fray.

By the time Brian moved out here, Alex and Ren, high school sweethearts, had been dating for a few years. Brian, Alex, Ren and I all went through university together, the boys renting an apartment in a house which Alex, through sheer financial savvy, eventually bought. A couple of years later, the house across the street from his became available at an unusually low price and even before we knew about it, Alex had convinced the owner –

a widowed, elderly man who was determined to have a young family inhabit his home – to sell it to us. And that is the house I live in now. The housing market distorted obscenely. Suddenly, we were homeowners in a city where owning a house implies that we are millionaires. Which we are not.

The overall effect is unsettling. I am still in the phase of explaining to my father why we live here at all, though it's been a decade and a half. The question of when we are moving back east rises to the surface of almost every conversation with him.

It's unfathomable to my father that there could be anywhere but Ontario. "Yes, except it rains so much," he complains, reflexively, after any statement I make that smacks of West Coast pride. To him, Ontario climate, seasons, topography are the standard and the West Coast a strange and fanciful deviation, not to be taken any more seriously than the idea of living in an amusement park. Yet, when he comes out to visit, he insists on high tea at the Empress, a ritual I can't believe still exists. Every time we make the march to the old hotel, I hope to see a sign telling us that at long fucking last the fading retiree resting place has given up the colonial ghost and wants to apologize for holding on for so absurdly long.

Back when we were students, we used to get around the city by bicycle, pedalling into the push of wind off the ocean, the full moon's reflection on the black water so luminous I would pretend the source of light came from below the surface. We used to go for slippery walks through the Chinese cemetery, scrabbling over the spongy moss on the ocean-shore rocks, falling quiet until we passed the graves. Our silence bloomed out of a warming feeling, a tender respect for a place so full of a weather-beaten peace. Time will pass, it seemed to say. And pass and pass, and pass again.

I think, much as I spent those first few years here falling in love with Brian, I was also falling in love with the city. (Or perhaps it's not falling in love, but falling into friendship – there ought to be a phrase for that.) Not falling for the city as people who have never lived here imagine it to be – the severely designed yet over-puffed gardens, the ridiculousness of peacocks in Beacon Hill Park, fish and chips, and wealthy, white conservatives – but with a damp layer beneath its presented face, the dank harbour stink, the green wet feel of the air, a cool, grey intimation of ghosts, mariners, salt, zonked-out hippies, the wild edges, and green-black water around every corner. There it is, the sea: constantly, soothingly seeping into my pores and making me amphibious, brine-bright, and lulled.

I bump my hip against Ren's old door and call hello as I enter. On my right, Ren is perched on the lip of the sofa in the living room, holding her one-year-old daughter, Juliette. Russell, her four-year-old, is in the corner smashing an action figure into a green truck.

Ren looks up and I notice her grey-green eyes are unusually large. Her right knee is quivering. She opens and closes her mouth, then opens her mouth again. "Russell was in the bath and I thought I'd just put Juliette in with him in for a minute. I, of course, meant to stay. But then I left, I can't even remember why; I think I had something in my hand to set down in the kitchen. I walked out and came back in and she was under the water, flail—" She stops. Her voice forcefully calm, snaps off. Our eyes lock; hers become wider.

I recognize immediately how she is feeling and how I must respond. It is what all of us are all doing here together, what we have become for each other.

"I've had that happen, too," I say evenly, though I have not. "We all have close calls sometimes." This is true. I've had near catastrophes, if not this one. The time the Dutch oven slipped from my soap-slick hands and carved a divot in the kitchen floor half an inch from Max's head.

I walk to the couch. I can smell her perfume, like green tea and grass. Ren is all pale green leaves with the light shining through – a ficus or a fern. Clean smells and a pliant, stem-like strength to her thinness.

Her eyes seem to lighten. "How many seconds was she under?" she asks me. "And how many seconds more would have…?"

"You walked in and out. That's not very many seconds at all. There's no need to beat yourself up, no need at all."

She stares at me, listening.

I smile to show that we can speak of the situation lightly. "It was probably only two or three seconds. Not enough time for anything to go wrong."

"But what if I'd become distracted and waited five or 10 or 30 seconds longer?"

"But you didn't," I say, and then realize that that's not what she needs to hear. I sit beside her on the couch, our babies immediately dip toward each other, lift fat fingers to fat fingers and make soft sounds at each other. "You wouldn't – you won't. You won't ever let yourself become that distracted with your kids."

She doesn't move and I say it again. "You won't." Her head tilts to the side, but her eyes don't follow. "You won't," I say once more.

At last, she breathes out and breaks off her stare. She jiggles Juliette on her knee. Juliette's face splits into a grin. God, what a face. Her two front teeth have come in with a magnetic, magnificent gap between them – like Madonna. "Good morning, Juliette," I say.

"I didn't even feel afraid at first. I just scooped her up and hugged her, dried her off. She barely coughed or cried. But the longer I sat there with her, the more I realized what could have happened, and then I tried to replay what I'd been thinking, what was in my hand that I needed to set down and where I'd set it down, and I couldn't. I still can't. A glass? All I can think of is what could have happened…a few more seconds, not even a minute. How can something so catastrophic and final happen so quickly? And so quietly?" She grips her daughter. Juliette pushes back, arching her body and writhing to one side with a little grunt.

"Ren, it's all right," I say. I have to keep talking until she slowly uncoils. But it's a while, 15 minutes or more of these waves, before I feel her emerge fully.

"Okay," she says, "okay," nodding at me. "Thank you for coming over."

"Any time," I say brightly, as though I've just brought her two eggs so she can complete a recipe. I know she's about to say something so I can leave if I want to – Ren always acts as though she feels she is either extending her welcome or holding onto people too long – so I say, "Coffee?"

She nods, looking relieved.

I've wanted to know Ren since I first met her. Back then she was quiet, a bit aloof, a long-distance runner studying art history. From a fairly well-off family that's been here for ages. She'd floated through university without having to think too much, while Brian and Alex and I had had to anchor our time there to a not-so-distant future in which we would need to remember how to speak in non-academic jargon, so we could channel our practical degrees into serviceable careers.

I think I know her a little now. Certainly, we are comfortable with each other. But she still keeps herself very privately wrapped. With Ren, everything's all right until it isn't. And then, without warning, everything goes wrong. There's that expression, You can't put the toothpaste back in the tube. Ren wants to believe that, at anytime, anything can be put back into itself. She is constantly pushing the paste back into the tube, quietly, resolutely.

"I saw Alex on his bike this morning," I say, placing Max on the rug in the living room in the spot where I know I will be able to see him from the counter that holds the Bodum.

Ren follows me to the kitchen. I can feel the way she floats, the softest of sounds, in the sleek, nude-coloured slippers she wears these days. Very French. Juliette calls out, "Dap! Dap!" and when I turn, eyes wide and smiling, she brightens: "Pllfff!"

Ren tucks her head into Juliette's curls and breathes deeply.

On the kitchen island, a paintbrush, its wooden stem splattered indigo, has dripped a few splotches of blue paint onto the floor.

So she had been painting – she's an artist now – had carried the brush to the bathroom, likely set it on the edge of the tub, put Juliette in the tub, then realized she still had the brush, and took it to the kitchen. But got to the kitchen and realized she shouldn't have walked away from Juliette, dropped the brush and rushed back.

Ren is looking at the brush, eyes locked on it.

I pick it up, run cold water over the bristles, carefully, as I have seen Ren do many times. I shake off the water, lay it on a towel beside the sink, swipe at the blue spots on the floor with a kitchen sponge, and begin making coffee.

Ren sits on a stool. "It's impossible," she says, not shaky now, but I can tell she is still upset, having moved past the fear of what almost happened to a puzzlement or bewilderment at herself, at life. "All the things to keep straight in my mind. I slide from thought to thought. There's so much to keep going, all at once." Suddenly, she looks at me, almost accusatorially. "You seem to keep everything intact. How do you do that?"

"Sticky notes," I say, half-joking. "A good pen. If I write it down in a list, I find I can keep ahead of it."

She frowns at me.

"I don't achieve half what I think I'm supposed to do," I say more seriously. "But the kids are safe, healthy, happy. Whatever happiness means to a one-year-old and two five-year-olds. And whatever safety and health is within my jurisdiction to provide."

She holds up her hand to me and I see she is vibrating. "I probably shouldn't drink any more coffee."

I stop measuring ground coffee into the delicate glass press, pause with the little silver scoop mid-air.

"Oh, you go ahead. I'll sit with you while you drink it." She waves her hand at me.

Russell comes to my side. "This guy's broken," he says, handing me the figure he'd been smashing earlier. It is some kind of Ken doll dressed in park ranger gear, a shiny slick of black hair carved into his plastic skull. There is a gaping cavity where one arm should be.

"Where's the arm?" I ask.

Russell shakes his head.

"I need an arm to fix it."

He turns and pads away.

Ren says: "What was it you were saying about Alex? You saw him this morning?" Something about the sound of her voice tells me she is fine again, or determined to be so. She is bouncing Juliette on her knees. They are framed by the breakfast nook window, the cherry tree outside; the window is open just enough to let in a soft breath of morning air. Juliette turns her head and shows me the gap in her teeth.

"It was just that I noticed something. In his back," I say.

Russell has returned. He holds out Park Ranger Ken in one fist and in the other, an arm, which is nearly the same size and shape though a different skin colour. I turn it over in my fingers. "Did you just pull this arm off Barbie?" I ask.

He nods solemnly. I look to Ren; she is staring hard at the broken doll, still bouncing Juliette, just slower. I press Barbie's arm into the gap in Park Ranger Ken's shoulder socket, and surprisingly, it snaps into place with a satisfying pop. I look to Ren again, to ask without saying, *Is this okay?* She gives the slightest nod and Russell retreats.

"What about it?" Ren clears her throat. "What about Alex's back?"

"I never noticed before. Does he have some kind of scoliosis or something? The way his back is…" Ren has stopped bouncing Juliette. She pulls her into her chest, gets off the stool and drifts to the edge of the living room to look in on the boys.

She doesn't say anything and doesn't look back at me.

"Russell, stop crashing your man into that truck." She sounds tense, tight. "I think it's time you should put that away." In her face, a kind of anguish. I see it from the side. One of the boys wails. It is Russ, responding to his mother.

"You know, Ren, I just remembered…I think I should get Max home." As I pick him up and walk to the door, I explain over my shoulder that he didn't sleep well, that he's due for a meltdown and I'd rather have it happen at our house.

I pause at the door. "I'm around the house all day," I say. "If you need—" I glance back at her, "that coffee, or anything, later."

It was a few years ago, before Juliette and Max, before Ren started selling her paintings and before a feature article appeared about her in *Vanguard*, a magazine that Brian makes fun of. "*Nouveau* Guard," he calls it and adds his own subhead: "Replacing colonialism with *riche* hipsterism one *faux* article at a time."

Back then, Ren wore plainer things. Well, plainer in a different way. Jeans and long-sleeved shirts. I guess that's much the same as what she wears now, but they fit her in a different way then. Less sculpturally, if that's the word? And her ponytails and buns were less sculptural as well. They just flopped around at the back of her head, caramel hair sprouting out of the elastic. I think perhaps she buys special elastics now.

Anyhow, it was when Russell was just a year old and my twins, May and Ruth, were two. We were at our house, out on the deck which back then was only half-built. The twins kept moving from the shed to the deck holding out their small fists to us, saying, "Here's chocolate," or, "Here's marshmallow kiss." It was ice cream parlour play. Ren and I stood talking, stooping to accept our ice cream cones.

"Oh, thank you," Ren said, holding an imaginary cone awkwardly.

"Excuse me," I said to May. "Does this marshmallow kiss ice cream have marshmallow in it?"

May puts one hand on her hip and looks up at me. "Just eat it, Mama." Behind her glare is a wicked smile. The two expressions are always duking it out for real estate on her face.

"It's just that—" I stick out my tongue and grimace, "Oh God. If you could just remove the marshmallow and keep the kiss, I'd be very happy."

She cracks. Leans right over in laughter. "Mama!"

A scream of tires, a throb of horn, a high-pitched yip. Ren's eyes moved to mine, confused.

"It's a dog," I say instinctively. "A dog's been hit. Ren, stay with the children."

I move so fleetingly to the street that I don't recall what I must have done: leapt over the pile of two-by-fours, told the twins to stay with Ren, opened the gate? In fact, Ren tells me later, I jumped the fence. I believe I must have done that, because I know what has happened before I get there. I know it is Judy, Alex's beloved yellow lab. I know that Judy is as much a part of Alex as Ren. I know that when we sit at a table, drinking beer, talking with our spouses, that Alex's hand drifts down and finds Judy's velvet head. When we used to camp together, as two young couples, Judy sat up front, between Ren (always in the passenger seat) and Alex (always the driver), and Judy was the first out the door, first into the ocean. Caught every stick he threw as though a bowline connected his arm to her teeth and throat. I know what I will see when I get to the side of the road and I also know that Ren cannot possibly handle the transactions that are about to follow.

When she does appear – the truck gone, the shaken postal worker who would not stop talking about his own dog, finally gone – it is almost an hour later. Brian and Alex are there because I have called them, instantly. Brian stays at our house with the kids, all of them; Alex and I wash our hands in his kitchen sink staring down into the gleaming metal drain and saying small sentences, little puffs of soothing steam.

"It was instant."

"Wouldn't have felt it."

"Had a long life."

"She was a good one."

After our hands are dry and we are walking back across the street – I think to collect the children and relieve Brian, I'm not sure we discussed a plan, it just seemed we should move across the street again – Ren appears at my gate. She looks confused. She holds herself in her arms.

"I'm very cold," she says to me. "I'll be back after I get a sweater." Then she looks at Alex and now I can see that she has been crying and is likely to start again. "Do you need a sweater from the house?"

He is wearing a windbreaker and underneath, his navy-blue sweater. "No, thank you," he says.

She glides past us (and it will be another hour or so before she's back, without the sweater – but who likes to cry in front of others?).

"She drifts sometimes," Alex says to me at the gate after she has gone.

I open my mouth to ask something, what does it mean to drift; why Ren? How careful do we need to be? If she is adrift, is there anyone to hold the other end of her line? But Alex moves swiftly up the front steps, takes all three at once, eager to be with his best friend, my husband, and his infant, those comforting creatures, now that his dog is gone.

This was before any babies. We were camping, sitting on drift-wood, smooth and worn, on a beach not far from the city. We were talking about our hometowns. Ren likes to hear stories about Ontario. To her, it's exotic territory. She's been to Toronto once or twice, but knows nothing of the small towns, of the "Soo," the Escarpment, Blue Mountains, Flowerpot Islands. She is fascinated by how much brick features in the architecture and by the invisible thin line that separates Ontario from Quebec. Every time we introduce a new shade or tone to her, she leans in.

"Algonquin Park," she repeats slowly after me, and for the first time I hear the word *Algonquin* and its lyrical beauty. "What's it like?"

"According to Erin's father, it's heaven," Brian says, and looks at me sideways, conspiratorially.

"Has he forgiven you yet?" Alex asks.

Brian snorts. "Has she moved back yet?"

Ren looks to me. "What's there to forgive? Doesn't he know you're happier here?"

I am thrown by her question and glad when a spark flies from the fire to distract us. It lands on Alex's jeans and he jumps up just as Judy leaps toward him.

"She's protecting you," Brian says, reaching out and stroking Judy's back.

Alex nods, and when he sits back down, pulls Judy to his chest. The damp fur smell of the dog and of Alex are inextricable. Even at a remove, I feel a certain calm watching how she eases him.

Ren stands and stretches. This is way back when she wore cargo pants and windbreakers, like the rest of us, when her hair had a haze of frizz to it, before she got it glossed and sleeked and carefully coloured to look as though she'd spent just the right amount of time, not in a salon, but in the sun.

After she mumbles goodnight, the three of us, and Judy, sit quietly, the night sifting toward us one shade at a time. I say to both men as though they are just one: "Do you think you are happier here?"

Brian twists his palm neatly over a beer bottle to remove the cap. He takes a swallow and passes me the bottle. "Sure. I mean, I think maybe *you* are. That's what you're getting at, right? You seem like you really belong here." He gazes at me, in deep concentration. "You're really part of it."

I look at him, amused. This is the kind of musing Brian only does when he is slightly stoned or lying in bed with me after sex. Or, when he is alone with Alex. This is a new understanding and I glaze into it. I can speak more freely with Alex now, I realize, when Brian is there. It will feel natural to us.

"But how would she know?" I ask. "She never knew me back home."

Alex leans back and smiles lazily. "That's the kind of thing Ren would say," he says. "She's from the West Coast; she thinks anyone would be happier here. She's like the only person I know who says she loves where she grew up."

"Erin's father," Brian mumbles. His eyes are half-closed. After a moment he says, "He would say the same thing. Don't you know Port Elgin is the best place in the world?" The end of his question is buried under a thick, soft stroke of sleepiness.

I turn to Alex. "Where do you say you grew up – here or there?"

He rakes his hand through Judy's fur. "I don't know. Doesn't matter. I grew up with my family. Doesn't matter where we were. Where Mom was, where Dad was, was home. Is."

I scratch at a mosquito bite behind my ear. "But sometimes you have to make your own home, away from your first home."

Alex sighs. "Erin, someday you'll have your own kids," he says. "What will you do if they want to grow up and move to Ontario?"

I laugh. Nobody who grows up on the West Coast dreams of moving to Ontario. We both know that. But I see that he is seriously putting the question to me, and I see why.

"Have to let them go," I say.

Alex slides down onto the sand, leans back and tilts his face toward the black sky. It is a warm night, and the breeze across our faces smells of deep sea. "Your dad," he says, and he shakes his head. "The only reason I can stand to live in the same city as my folks is that they never asked me to stay."

When I get back home that morning, the phone is ringing in my kitchen. I jump for it wondering if I left Ren too soon.

"Erin? Ernie, it's Dad. I'm calling with some shitty news. Really shitty, pissy news."

Brian wipes counters, stacks Tupperware in the fridge, walks by the table and takes Max from my arms, goes upstairs and comes back down, fills two glasses of water at the sink but watches me, goes back up and comes back down.

He stands in front of me. The skin under his eyes plum-coloured and sheeny. God. Brian. This good and ever-appealing man. "Did he say anything about looking into alternative treatments? Acupuncture or TCM or anything?"

"Brian. It's my dad."

"But it might help with the pain."

"My dad. The guy who thinks massage therapy is 'new age.' He'll take the scary drugs they give him and keep on eating fried steak for breakfast."

Brian groans, his head dropping back. "Fuck. The world just keeps on turning around him, doesn't it? He will not be moved."

"He will not be moved," I repeat slowly, and Brian sits beside me, as quickly as he can, with Max asleep in the sling on his chest.

"We'll do whatever you need to do. If we need to spend some time in Ontario…"

Something about the word Ontario, the homing sound of it, releases the loosened pin. I dissolve in the worst, slobbery, salty way. "We should've gone back so long ago. That's all he really wanted. He just wanted us close. I had to be so sure that I needed to be here. How would I ever survive it if our kids wanted to move away from here to go live back east?"

"Ah, Erin." Brian leans toward me, and Max's head lolls to the side. He hugs me as best he can. "Nobody who grows up here ever wants to move to Ontario."

I make one of those awful, weirdly comical wailing sounds that is both crying and laughing. "We'll have to stay here forever," I sob. And Brian laughs.

I reach up and loosely hang my fingers in Brian's fingers, take a breath. I remember then what I was planning to tell him before my dad called. I wipe at my cheeks with the heels of my hands.

"Does Alex have some kind of back or shoulder problem?"

Brian squints. "Huh?"

"I noticed like a, like a stoop, or a hunch, this morning—"

"Are you kidding me?"

"Like a thing," I reach behind and touch my back.

"You just noticed this?"

"Has he had it forever?"

"Well, for—" Brian looks up to the ceiling, "16 years? There was an accident, but I don't know the details. It was when they were in high school. They were driving somewhere late at night. I don't know anything else. They won't talk about it."

"They?"

Brian looks at me, bewildered. "He and Ren. Neither one will say a word. I can't believe you never noticed it before."

"I guess I noticed, but never thought about it being *something*. I just thought he was shaped that way."

Brian shakes his head. "I love that about you," he says and leans in, lays his head on my shoulder. "You're oblivious to all the right things."

I move so that his head bumped off my shoulder. "I'm not oblivious." I glower at him. "What else am I oblivious to?"

"I didn't mean – it was a compliment."

"That doesn't sound complimentary."

"I meant…you don't care about pretences that don't really matter."

"Like what kind of pretences?"

Max stirs and Brian shushes him, stands and begins bouncing on the balls of his toes. "It's not an insult," he says, "it's just like, you don't care about appearances like some people do. Like—" he looks around, and his eyes land on the window, "you know, the way Ren has become."

I frown, surprised to find a knee-jerk loyalty. "What's wrong with the way she's become?"

Brian looks at me as though he thinks I may not be serious. "The expensive clothes, the abstract painting, the Danish furniture? She wasn't into that stuff before, when Alex first met her. He doesn't care about any of that."

"They were teenagers when they met," I say. "Of course she wasn't who she would become. You're not even a fully formed human being when you're a teenager." My eyes flit out the window and across the street to their house. "Does it bother him?"

Brian's eyes widen. "Um, yeah. Of course it bothers him. A lot. I can't believe you haven't noticed."

I turn to him sharply. "Hey. Go easy. You're the one who just said you liked me for my lack of observational abilities."

"That's – okay, that is not what I said."

I hold out a hand. "I'm not mad, I just – I don't think that's fair of Alex. Ren has changed a lot – so what? Aren't we all allowed to change?"

"Yeah, I guess so," Brian frowns. "Is this – are you just upset about your dad and channelling it into this conversation?"

I glare at him.

"Okay! It's just that I didn't think you'd be so loyal to Ren. I always thought it bothered you a little, how she's become. You know, we bought these houses and all of a sudden we all started making a little more money and Ren just kind of veered off in a funny direction, acting rich or something, but the rest of us never did."

"Acting rich!" I hoot, as though it were a ridiculous thing to say. Truth is, I have thought the same in my own curious way – what does it mean to live in these houses, in this city? Are we acting rich, just by not being homeless here? Does Ren do this with a bit more awareness than the rest of us, puts on the costume?

"I don't think you should judge a person just because she likes nice things," I say.

"I'm not—"

"Yeah, you are. And Alex is, too. He's always been bothered by how much money her family has. Well, how is that any better than looking down on someone for not having any? She is the way she is, okay? She loves Alex and her kids; she paints. She's just trying to do what it feels right for her to do."

"Okay. I wasn't—"

"People aren't supposed to stay the same, Brian. It's not about staying in the same place with someone. You should be able to change as much as you want and know that the other person is still connected to you."

Brian caresses Max's head, watching me.

"Maybe it is a little weird, some of the things she does," I continue, "but it's worse what Alex has become, if he's going to let her go just because of it. He's supposed to hang on, no matter what."

Brian keeps caressing Max's head. He doesn't say anything. I know from many years of arguments and conversations with this man that he has come to the point, which means I have also come to the point, where we realize I just have some things I have to say. And somehow, he is willing to take it. He is always somehow willing.

I heave a deep sigh, Brian watching me. He says, "I don't see anyone letting go of anyone in this situation."

"Even Alex and Ren?" I ask.

"Well, that I can't answer."

He comes over and stands close. I look at him from the corner of my gaze, meet his eyes, which look sleepy yet attuned, full of the open-handed care Brian manages to dole out tirelessly.

He pulls me to my feet and walks me through the kitchen, turning out the lights behind us, guiding me upstairs, and down the hallway, to the bedroom. When I sit on the bed and sink my weight against the pillows, he pulls my leg across his lap, peels off my sock.

We watch the doing of these things, with Max nuzzled against Brian's chest; the familiar hushing sound of rain against the windows begins, or perhaps it has been there and I've only just noticed it. It occurs to me: not only what a soothing sound this rain is, but also how it has become the sound of our lives, and maybe, I think, maybe this is what I want the sound of the rest of my life to be, and I think how fortunate I am to be in the place that has the right sound for me. The right feel of dampness, the right colourations. For me.

And then in the next moment, I stop hearing the rain because I am hearing the loop of what I should have done, how I should be, and why I am here not there, where my father obviously needs me, and always has.

Brian leans forward suddenly and touches my forehead. "Shhhh," he says. "Stop doing that to yourself, please."

I wake up at 4:51 in the morning. A ridiculous time to wake – too early to get out of bed, too late to fall back to sleep. Max is between Brian and me in the bed, his arms flung over his head, knees flopping to each side. Brian's mouth hangs open, the grey duvet peaks and valleys around his head. Rain dribbles against the window. These moments are perhaps the finest offerings in my life: one or more of my children asleep beside my sleeping husband, the sound of rain, the possibility of a coffee drunk quietly and alone in the kitchen. It will be 8:00 back home, I realize. Dad will be up, sipping his Folgers, black, one sugar, sitting at the kitchen table. I reach for my cell phone and walk silently downstairs, sit at the window bench at our kitchen table and look out across the street.

I am, of course, staring at Ren's house. But I don't notice that this is what I am doing until a sudden movement on the porch rouses my eyes. It's Ren, in jeans and a long grey sweater, stepping out the door. She pulls the sweater tight around her and lifts her chin as though smelling the air, then steps down from the front porch and walks across the yard, toward her studio. Walking this way brings her closer to our window, maybe 20 feet from where I sit, but her head is angled down. Then suddenly, she lifts her face and looks right at me. We jolt. I raise a hand slowly and Ren gazes at me. After a moment, she beckons. I look behind me, stupidly, as though there could be anyone else, then I nod eagerly and rush through our front hallway and out the door.

The damp air washes over me. I haven't been outside so early in a while and I had forgotten. That medicinal early air of the west. It's as though the ocean reclaims the city over each night. There's a great, rushing quietude and a seaweed smell. It lies thickly, comfortingly over everything. I resist the impulse to move my hands, brush the air from side to side as I move through it, the green scent coating my skin, my face, my hands. Ren is watching me cross the street, and as I get close to her she nods.

"It's so quiet you can smell better," she says. "Isn't that it?"

I nod.

"It's even better when it's raining this time of day. You can hear the drops landing on the leaves."

"Mmm."

"I find, now that we have children, quiet like this is…" she looks around, searching, "…exquisite. It's where I suddenly know what to paint. Look," she points at the canopy of cherry branches and blossoms above us. The power lines cutting through the pink lace of them and just above, a gauze of clouds like a cotton puff pried and pried apart until it is just wisps. The sun has infused the clouds a pale pink so that it appears we are looking up into layers of rose, blush, raspberry, and cream.

I look at her looking up. Usually, whenever I see Ren, she is wearing makeup. Minimalist though it may be, to see her skin as it is now, uncovered, feels intimate. A tiny spider vein squiggles to the right of the bridge of her nose. This is the kind of thing she would take care to cover up – with the kind of concealer that is so expensive as to be undetectable. And the signs of sleepiness under her eyes, the lovely hollows tinted lavender. Her hair, strands of it falling loose around her face.

"I don't mean I find them too noisy," she continues. "Or distressing." She shakes her head at me. "I find having children so…painfully wonderful." She looks at me and smiles a helpless sort of smile. "People say, it goes so fast. They'll be grown before you know it. But I find the opposite. They've slowed my life down so much because I have to be in it every moment of every day. They've forced me to be aware of each passing second." She looks at me. "I can't seem to get myself to take them for granted. It's the best thing anyone's ever done for me – and it's an excruciating way to live." She holds my gaze and then shrugs.

"I know."

She holds my eye for a moment longer and then shifts her weight, about to move on, but stops. "I heard about your dad. Brian called Alex last night." She tips her head at me. "I'm so sorry, Erin. I know how much you worry about him already."

I screw up my mouth, find myself swallowing hard.

"Erin."

I kick at the ground with the toe of my sneaker. "I'm all he has." I look up at the branches, blinking back tears. "Do you think it's awful of me? Shouldn't I have stayed where he was all along? It was just him and me, my whole life, I really never should have left—"

"Stop," Ren says. She says it gently. She waits and we just stand there, me looking up at the sky and Ren looking at me. After a moment she says, "You're a good daughter, Erin. It shouldn't matter where."

The house is still sleeping when I walk back through the front door, up the steps into the kitchen. I stand at the window with my cell phone.

"Oh. Dad, it's me. I didn't think I'd get your answering machine." I look dumbly at my feet, my voice gone flat. "Listen. I wanted to tell you – I just wanted to say…" I stop and take a breath. "I know you don't want to move out here to let me help take care of you. And you know I can't move my family back to Ontario." I pause, close my eyes. "But I wanted to tell you that wherever we are, I'm the person on the other end of this line. Okay? There's a line that connects you and me, and wherever you are, I'm the one on this end of it. I never let go of that line." My throat constricts. I hang up the phone, swallow, and look out the window.

Across the street, Ren and Alex's door is opening, and Alex appears. I glance at the clock. Of course: it's Friday morning, almost 6:30. Brian and Alex have a standing date to walk to work together one morning a week, a holdover from their university days when they would walk from this street, through the city, to campus together, philosophizing or making ridiculous jokes or whatever it is the two of them love to do so much together. Alex is crossing the street, looking to our window, and he throws up an arm in greeting when he sees me.

"Sorry about your dad," he says as he walks in the front door. "You doing okay?"

I shrug. He punches me in the shoulder, and cocks his head.

"You're doing okay," he says, full of certainty and looking me in the eye, as though by saying this he makes it true. "Oh, and I wanted to say thanks to you for coming over yesterday, after—" He frowns. "…after Ren got upset. She told me how you helped."

"I really didn't do anything."

"Just being available," he says, "is what helps her, I think. Just knowing she can call you."

"I'm not worried," I say.

Alex gives me a look. "That's good, I guess."

I realize something then: I don't doubt Ren's capability. That she fades in and out does not alarm me. If it did, I'd make more excuses to be around. I'd make myself more present in their home. Alex would understand. He would expect it. He's even waiting for it right now, maybe.

But Ren is all right. She is of a kind, here. A kind of West Coast woman. They move encapsulated in their own mist, styled with precision to convey a certain windblown beauty, a belonging, a status, and a place. She's never had to sharpen her focus; a soft gaze has served her well, mostly. But having children inverses so many of our qualities.

I do believe what I told her, that she won't ever drift too far. She loves her kids, *to distraction*, as the old saying goes. But with Ren it's all been distraction. Until now. She loves them to a converging point. Her scope is honing in, and in. She sees them through a periscope, as though out at sea. One day she'll lower the glass and they'll be right there in front of her, affixed to her through her unceasing seeing.

Brian's voice comes suddenly from above: "Alex here?"

"Hurry up, sloth!" Alex shouts back.

Brian's voice again: "Stop showing up early!"

"Get a watch!"

Alex and I meet eyes and grin. It's a familiar exchange, the words frayed and worn at the edges in a pleasing way. I feel my eyes move over his neck and shoulders and he, noticing, unbends his posture, or tries to.

"Does it hurt?" I ask him.

He raises his eyebrows, surprised. "More than it used to," he says in a conceding tone, as though he has not wanted to admit this to himself.

"Well," I say, taking a step forward. Above me, I hear the thundering sound of two five-year-olds waking and Brian thumping along the hallway, down the stairs. I touch Alex on the shoulder lightly, right at the place where it seems an old bend has deepened.

It occurs to me that Alex is not just my husband's friend, not just my friend, and not just Ren's husband. He is certainly all of these, but there is another part to him as well. He is like a man made of folded paper, and I have just uncreased another corner and I see him becoming a new shape in front of me.

We are opposite ends, he and I, of a love for Ren, a love for Brian. Should his end go slack, it's up to me to make up the equipoise.

"Well, we all have our soft spots," I tell him.

He laughs. "Right."

"Sometimes I think we have these gaps in ourselves so that others have a place to fit into."

Alex watches me, showing a sort of confusion, and a pain.

Brian bursts into the hallway. "I'm not late! You're seven minutes early. Seven!" I have poured him a Thermos of coffee and left a nectarine beside it on the counter. He dashes to me, the thermos in hand and stoops to give me a running kiss before jamming the nectarine in his mouth and setting the coffee down, shrugging his jacket on, glaring playfully at Alex. He's out the door first, shouting something, and Alex leans to pull at the doorknob, to close it behind them. He pauses just before it's closed and sticks his head back in. He reaches for Brian's Thermos from the bench by the door and then glances outside as Brian repeats whatever it is he has been shouting.

Alex looks at me: "He says I love you, and thank you. And see you," then closes the door.

THE CRITICS

When they were kids, Audrey and Skyla liked to put on shows. Skyla had a super-symmetrical Shirley Temple face, with metallic green eyes and a button-mushroom nose. She'd been the kind of child who delighted adults with her willingness to perform. "A doll," Audrey's mother, Barb, often called her. You could ask Skyla to sing a song from the choir, and she would, adding jazz hands or a cocked hip for flair.

The shows consisted of corralling their parents into dining room chairs while the girls dressed up and fluttered around, playing background music on the stereo, talking up a performance which they had scantly planned. Often there were capes, batons, glitter, and lipstick. At some point, they sang.

When Skyla was in front of their parents performing, Audrey stood behind her, mouthing the words, her arms glued to her sides. She saw the look on her mother's face, total rapture when she watched Skyla, and a coaxing, pleading look for Audrey. "What a card!" Barb would say, later on, when Skyla's teenage quips and snarks were just the right combination of sugar and salt.

Skyla's mother, Lesley, usually didn't make it through the shows. She'd sit frowning, as though trying to sort out how she'd ended up there, then excuse herself, saying she had to get some work done. That's when Skyla would bring out the big guns: a cartwheel that ended in somewhat painful-looking splits.

Later, as teenagers, the two girls' families went on trips together from Halifax to Boston or Toronto, and their parents let the girls go off on their own for an afternoon. Audrey's mother, who fretted over her children, seemed to think Audrey was safe as long as she was with Skyla, while Skyla's mother expected smart behaviour at all times and assumed Audrey would keep Skyla in line. The girls failed on both accounts: within moments Audrey would become flustered and disoriented. Skyla had a way of leading her around, making jokes about the scariness of subways, lingering around the doorways to bars, or even strip clubs, just to make a nervous Audrey laugh.

That was when they invented the Game: following people around, criticizing or adoring their clothing, guessing at their lives, daring each other to talk to a stranger. Audrey never did, but Skyla would saunter up to anyone, and she once took a cigarette out of a man's mouth, putting it in her own.

"How do you do that?" Audrey asked her.

"Easy." Skyla shrugged. "It's just a game."

Skyla and Audrey lived together their last year of university at Dalhousie. They had a roommate, Kaitlyn, who announced at the end of spring semester that in a few weeks she was taking a train from the east coast to the west. Audrey glanced up from her cornflakes and coffee. "The West Coast?"

Neither Audrey nor Skyla had made post-graduation plans – the general pattern was that once Skyla had made a major life decision, Audrey's would follow. But Skyla had been avoiding the topic and seemed reluctant even to say which of her electives – English, theatre, psychology – most interested her.

The words "Vancouver" and "train" struck a bell in Audrey's head and she found herself imagining sitting at a train window with a hardcover novel in her lap, curving through the landscape into a mist of mammoth trees.

Skyla, with her sharp green irises, scanned Audrey's face.

"You don't have the balls," Skyla said, and Audrey blinked.

"For what?"

"I know what you're thinking. There's no way you could do something like that." Skyla smiled brightly at Kaitlyn. "But how fun for you, Kaitlyn."

Audrey stirred cream into her coffee. Across the table, Kaitlyn buttered her toast. When Skyla dumped her dishes in the sink with a clatter and left, shouting over her shoulder that she'd be sleeping at her parents', Kaitlyn said: "Watch out for her. She's got it in for you."

Audrey startled: "She's just…like that sometimes. Skyla and I have been friends since we were three. We're practically family."

"So what?"

Audrey sipped her coffee and looked the other way, her chin slightly lifted, slowly, as though she'd been asked a question too absurd to answer. She'd seen Grace Kelly make this move in a film when someone's remark threw her for a loop. *So what, indeed*, she was thinking. Was it possible being best friends at three and 13 didn't add up to being friends at 23? Why hadn't she thought to ask herself this before?

A few days later, Audrey announced she was joining Kaitlyn on the train. She got dizzy thinking about it. *Go west for the summer*. And do what? She wasn't sure. And be there all alone? *Yes!* She kept sipping sparkling water to settle her stomach, but now that she'd said it, she couldn't retract it. And didn't want to. The idea was like a cultured pearl in the palm of her hand that she was slowly closing her fingers around.

In Audrey's bedroom in the apartment they shared, Skyla sat on the bed, crunching carrot sticks, watching Audrey pack.

"I was thinking I might move to Toronto in the fall." *Crunch.* "I'm just saying, don't count on me being here when you get back. I was thinking of just going for the summer, but what's the point? A summer's nothing."

Audrey smoothed out a cardigan, folding it in a neat square before placing it in her suitcase. She did a mental check: clothes for warm weather, rain, job interviews, spontaneous dates. "Aren't you applying to med school?"

Skyla flung herself backward on the bed dramatically, growling, "I'm sick of talking about med school!"

Audrey rolled a braided leather belt into a tight coil. "Your mom's just trying to help. She doesn't think you're motivated about pursuing anything else—"

Skyla barked out a laugh. "Thanks for telling me what my own mom thinks about me."

"Well," Audrey pressed her lips together and looked around the room. "What is it that you want to do?" It felt risky to ask this of Skyla. She'd never said what she wanted to be and there was a hard shell around the topic as though it was something too delicate to speak of. There had been a time when Skyla confided in her, but that was beginning to seem like a long time ago.

Skyla touched at a large pimple on her chin, absently, and then turned to bury her face in a pillow. Just as quickly, she shot up, grabbed another carrot stick, and pretended to smoke it like a cigarette – not in a juvenile way, but in a convincing, cinematic way – while peering into Audrey's suitcase. "God, you pack like my grandmother. Making sure you have an outfit for every occasion." She blew imaginary smoke from the corner of her lips. "What's this one for?" She pulled out a pencil skirt and crisp blouse from the bottom of the stack, upsetting everything parcelled out on top of it.

Audrey pressed her lips. "Museums."

Skyla threw her head back, laughing. Carrot flew from her mouth. "Well, don't forget your pearls! Seriously, Kaitlyn's old aunt will be thrilled to have a new best friend."

Audrey flicked the bit of carrot from the top of her travel jewellery case. "I'm not staying with Kaitlyn and her aunt in Vancouver. I'm going on my own to Victoria."

In a high school textbook there had been pictures of the old Victoria hotel, The Empress; she'd wanted to go to Victoria ever since. It seemed like a place with an aesthetic that was polished and regal. She imagined meeting someone in the lobby – the carpet would be plush underfoot. She'd wear an A-line skirt and kitten heels – with no Skyla there to make fun of her preference for classic fashion.

She was aware of Skyla gawping at her, and felt a ripple of satisfaction.

But then Skyla hauled herself up off the bed and stood so close to Audrey their toes touched. "You won't last two weeks on your own. You're too afraid of everything."

She wanted to say, "I'm not, anymore," but it wasn't quite true and her throat suddenly felt thick. She stood looking at Skyla's face, so intimately familiar to her, and thinking how, up this close, all she could see were the blemishes.

Audrey's dad and Skyla's mother were doctors at the hospital. That was how the two families first met. Skyla had grown up in a turreted Victorian near Point Pleasant Park, the expensive end of Halifax. To get into their yard, Audrey had to punch a code into a wrought-iron gate. Skyla's mother, Lesley, wore high heels that tick-tocked on the shiny floors. Audrey marvelled at her hair – a bold, premature white, cut with razor-precision in an angle across her forehead. She was not exactly warm.

Audrey's mother, Barb, on the other hand, had shoulder-length, butterscotch hair that she wore in a butterfly clip, half up, half down. She was usually in slippers and hand-knit sweaters. Seemingly content, she had been a stay-at-home mom, taking care of Audrey and her five brothers and sisters with craft projects, park outings, and baking. The house was full of rockets made from paper towel rolls, paper plates stuck with glitter and spiral pasta, now many years old. Skateboards, hockey sticks, paperbacks, clarinet and violin cases had settled on top of the first layer of debris. Barb kept it all. She loved scrapbooking; she cried when one Mother's Day she discovered the family had secretly converted a walk-in closet into "Scrapbook Head-quarters" (this is what the sign on the door read). More often than not, Barb forgot to ask Audrey how school was going and when Audrey told her she wanted to do her master's, her mother seemed a bit perplexed.

"For what?"

Audrey, home for dinner, was sitting at the kitchen table with her mother, father, and the three brothers who were still in high school She was leaving in the morning for Victoria on the train.

"English."

"No," Barb said, "I mean, what do you need a master's for?"

"Well, it would help me get a better job for one thing. But for another, I want to keep studying literature."

Barb, salad bowl in hand, seemed to be mulling over Audrey's words.

"Well, I think it is a fine idea," Audrey's dad said. "You should check out the universities in Victoria and Vancouver this summer."

"You wouldn't move all the way out there, though, dear. Would you, Audrey? I thought this was just a little trip. For the summer? You can do a master's here – can't you?"

Audrey leaned back and crossed her legs. "I might move out there," she said, a trill of nervousness running through her.

"But there's no family out there," Barb protested. "Where will you go for Thanksgiving dinner?"

Audrey looked at her mother, floral oven mitts on both hands and an apron that said WILL COOK FOR KISSES. Home-cooked meals, family gatherings, recipes, household chores, and the occasional stolen moment to watch *The View* or read her *Shopaholic* books – Audrey saw her mother's day clearly. If they'd been playing their game, Audrey thought, Skyla would have said: "Housewife," in a tone that meant that *housewife* is not a thing to be proud of. Or perhaps, Audrey realized with discomfort, that was how she saw her own mother. Skyla had never criticized Barb; if and when Audrey complained about her mother, Skyla just listened.

Then Audrey thought of Lesley, Skyla's mother: assertive, imperious, sharp. What would Skyla have called her? "CEO," Audrey would have said, meaning *powerful*. What Skyla would say came to Audrey a moment later: ice queen or, possibly, bitch.

Her mother was still staring at her, mouth hanging open in a way that annoyed Audrey. "Honey? Why would you move all the way out there?"

"To. Study. Literature," Audrey said, as though she were talking to a child. Her dad shot her a sharp look and she dropped her eyes to her plate, knowing she should feel guilty.

Audrey hadn't grown into her length until they'd started university, about the same time she'd stopped hiding behind her bangs. Her figure became less stick-like and more lithe, making everything she wore look interesting, distinctive. She developed a look for reserved, well-tailored clothes – a look she admired in old film noir movies – and soon other girls tried mimicking her style.

Skyla, on the other hand, had puffed out after she started university. And then, quite suddenly, Skyla's face bloomed with acne – the angry-looking kind. It started as a trail of pus-filled whiteheads along her chin and then spread all over her face, exploding into oily red mounds, leaving pockmarks where she picked at them. When she tried to cover them up, it looked like she'd spackled beige cottage cheese onto her cheeks.

Lesley was a dermatologist, but she hadn't taken much interest in Skyla's battle with her face. "Smarten up," is what Lesley said to Skyla's young adult sass. Her skin got worse and worse.

Around the time they graduated from Dalhousie, it was Barb – noticing how the acne crippled Skyla's confidence – who bought Skyla a skincare kit she'd seen advertised on TV. The box promised a clear, radiant complexion.

Skyla looked at the kit. "Results in six months," she read flatly.

Barb put her arm around Skyla's hunched shoulders. "I know it seems like a long time, dear, but—"

Skyla looked up. "Six months," she said again, her whole face changing, illuminating. "I can do six months." She leaned into Barb's arm.

Around the same time, as Audrey learned to roll her shoulders back and lift her chin, Lesley began to take notice of her. A few weeks before leaving for Victoria, Audrey dropped by the big house to visit Skyla. Lesley was at the dining-room table where she often worked. She leaned back in her chair, and Audrey could feel her watching as she crossed the foyer. Lesley called: "Audrey. "

Audrey was wearing a black turtleneck, slim on her slender figure, and black pants cropped above her small, smooth ankle bones, black ballet flats. It was an Audrey Hepburn day. Lesley studied her a moment, her glasses off, but held between one finger and thumb. "Have you given any consideration to law or political science. Journalism?"

Audrey rolled the question around in her mind, pleasantly. "I like reading best. I've tried to write my own stories, but it doesn't come naturally."

"What do you like about reading exactly?"

Again, the question was like a treat. She savoured it before responding, "I like picking a story apart. Deciding for myself whether it's…effective or not." She was pleased at choosing a more erudite word than *good*.

Lesley nodded, the architectural bangs grazing one high cheekbone. "What do you consider effective in contemporary American literature?" And so on, until Audrey had been sitting there for 45 minutes, dissecting Roxane Gay, Lauren Groff, Rebecca Solnit. Skyla, coming downstairs to find Audrey with her mom, was agitated.

"What the hell were you two talking about?" she asked as Audrey followed her back upstairs.

"Female voices in American literature and their effect on—"

Skyla halted. "No school talk outside of school, remember?"

On her last night in Halifax, Audrey went to a friend's house for a party. It was a going-away party for Audrey and Kaitlyn. Josh was there – he and Skyla had dated earlier in the year, Audrey having a crush on him all the while. But after things cooled between Josh and Skyla, Audrey never quite got up the courage to ask him out. Or rather, she'd never had the nerve to ask Skyla if it was okay to ask him out.

Skyla got drunk in a drinking game. Audrey took little sips of her wine cooler and Skyla snorted.

"Look at Little Miss Priss over there." She took a swig of beer with her pinky finger sticking out. "Oh, I would never get smashed!" she exclaimed in dramatic modesty, in a British accent for flair. A few people laughed in a sort of uncommitted way, but Josh frowned and set his unfinished drink down on the table and went into the kitchen. "Come dance with me, Audrey!" he called over his shoulder.

Audrey had a look of surprise – Skyla went on with the act, changing her accent to Southern belle: "Who? Li'l ol' me?" she asked, fluttering her eyelashes and pressing her fingers to her chest. But she elbowed someone's beer bottle while doing it and drew back from the splash. "Fuck! I'm all gross now! Thanks a lot, Audrey." She got up without wiping the beer or apologizing and everyone around the table looked at each other awkwardly before wandering into the kitchen.

Josh was dancing the way a funny uncle or kindergarten teacher might, not trying to look cool, just wanting to make Audrey laugh, and it was working. As she slid from her perch on the counter to join him, Skyla came grinding up behind Josh, pushing her hips into his ass, but still making a puckered-lip ingenue face, holding her pinky out. "Oh my! Look at me, every-one! I'm touching a man's bum!" She cracked into sharp laugh-ter, looking around for someone to join her.

Someone turned the music up and then they couldn't hear her.

A little later, they walked home, Skyla lurching in clunky high heels. "Imagine how huge a zit would look on the big screen," she slurred, leaning into Audrey and then laughing as though she'd made a joke. Her eyes searched Audrey's.

"What?" Audrey asked, reaching out to steady her.

"The film of the year," Skyla said in movie voice-over, "star-ring… Skyla Roberts's acne." She snickered and tottered.

Audrey looked at her friend and for the first time saw what the acne was doing to her. "Skyla—"

"Remember the Game, Audrey?" Skyla asked suddenly. "What would we say about me now?" She laughed sharply and then said nothing the rest of the way.

The next morning Audrey tapped on Skyla's door, lightly, but heard no answer, just the phlegmy sound of hangover snor-ing.

Somewhere in Manitoba, on the train west, Kaitlyn brought it up. They were sharing a pot of tea and a bag of M&Ms. Or rather, Kaitlyn was munching on the candy; Audrey picked the occasional one out of the bag and sucked on it. Kaitlyn said, "Skyla told me you said I was getting fat."

"You are not fat, Kaitlyn."

Kaitlyn shrugged. "But did you say it?"

Audrey paused, her teacup partway to her mouth. "*No*," she said. "Of course not."

"So then why'd Skyla say you did?"

"She really said that?"

"Yeah. And you know what else? Skyla told Emily that you said she wore cheap, shitty clothes and looked like a homeless person."

Audrey glared. "What? When?"

"And she told Ivy that you said the hair on her head looks like pubic hair."

Audrey almost laughed except she could see how serious Kaitlyn was. "When did all this happen?"

"Recently. I told you…she has it in for you." There was a glint in Kaitlyn's eye that caught Audrey's attention. She wasn't making it up, Audrey thought, but she was enjoying delivering the news.

"I would never say those things."

It hadn't started that way, but the Game had become cruel. When they had played, sitting in a pub in Halifax, or attending a big event on campus, Skyla would say: "That guy, he's a tech freak. Lives in a basement and masturbates all day. And she's a 40-year-old single woman who can't get a date; she watches *Legends of the Fall* while eating raw cookie dough, like twice a week."

Skyla's crassness unnerved Audrey, but at the same time, it felt like a challenge. She tried her hand at it: "He wears mom jeans. She paid twenty bucks for her haircut." But Skyla would snicker at her and call her a prude. Audrey had no gift for zingers – she couldn't say words like "masturbate" or "porn," not as naturally as Skyla – but she was good at critiquing. She studied people and often wished she could give them advice: cover your roots; don't wear Gore-Tex when you're not camping; learn how to hold a fork; try not to use slang, and never ever pass gas in front of others.

But she never said things like that about people they knew. Only strangers. Skyla had told Audrey that Emily was a bad dresser and Audrey had thought to herself, *She looks cheap*. And with Ivy, too, Skyla had laughed when their friend had walked away and whispered to Audrey, "That haircut looks hideous on her." And Audrey had thought, just *thought*, to herself: *Her hair is too dark and wiry for that cut.*

If Skyla knew she thought those things, did she also know what Audrey was thinking about her, now? That she was glad Skyla had gotten acne – the blow that rearranged their pecking order – and that she was glad Skyla never had her kind of conversations with Lesley.

Audrey had arranged a house-sit and part-time job in Victoria through a family connection. She spent her first evening organizing the house, putting things into cupboards in tidy lines and stacks. She could hear Skyla in her ear: "Oh, lighten up, Audrey. You're so anal." Audrey hated the word. "Bum" she could take, but "anal" made her think of colonoscopies and hemorrhoid cream.

Her job at the bookstore started three days after she arrived in Victoria. She could have taken the bus, but she preferred to walk. The differentness of the West was a revelation to her. The air felt clean and mossy in her nose, her skin became dewy and her hair puffed up, but she tamed it, shiny and straight, into a glossy ponytail.

On her walk that morning, Audrey felt a pang for Skyla – the old Skyla. They would have followed the woman in front of them in her high-heeled boots, a leather clutch under her arm, a trench coat cinched tightly around a thin figure, wondering what her story was.

"Fashion designer," Audrey would have said.

"Stockbroker by day, stripper by night."

Or Skyla might have said something more cutting, and Audrey would have had to sort out that uncomfortable feeling that lay somewhere between disapproval and thrilling agreement.

She said to Josh on the phone one evening, "I just wanted to make sure you knew I didn't say those things."

"Everybody who knows you, knows those are Skyla's words, not yours. You're the nice one, Audrey. Have you talked to her?"

"No."

"Well, good. You know, I love the old Skyla, but this new one's a bully. She's just jealous of you and making you pay for it."

Audrey blanched, a sudden fizz in her stomach. "She couldn't be jealous of me." But she realized as she said it that she was trying to draw him out, and Josh walked right into it, assuring her for the next few minutes that she had bypassed Skyla in likeability and coolness.

"Would you even be friends with her if your families weren't so close?" he asked.

She swallowed, unsure how best to respond.

"I mean, I get that you two have history," he said, "but if you met her today for the first time, honestly, what would you think of her?"

She selected the words carefully, knowing Josh didn't go for mean, and yet, here was the chance to throw the stone to sink the ship. "I think I'd feel sorry for her."

Josh was quiet for a moment and she felt her stomach twist – perhaps she'd laid it on too thick. But then he said, "See? Even when you have a right to be angry, you're still nice."

It is *easy*, she thought.

By the time she hung up the phone, her stomach hurt and her teeth ached, like she'd indulged in too much candy.

The bookstore where she worked part-time was busy. The manager, Lee, a quirky but focused businesswoman and bibliophile, took a liking to Audrey. She noticed when Audrey reorganized a section so that it displayed better or knew exactly what book to recommend to a customer. She agreed to write a reference letter for Audrey's University of Victoria grad studies application, and in it had called Audrey *eloquent, discerning,* and *refined.* Lovely words. She kept rolling them through her mind like ticker tape.

"You've got great taste," she said to Audrey one grey August day, when Audrey had been there three months. Audrey was structuring a display of Young Adult reads, bypassing the popular vampire-witch-and-wizard fare for classics.

"Lee, I saw a photograph at Delia's place where I'm house-sitting. It showed her in front of a big sign that said CLARION BOOKS. Is that another bookstore in town?"

"That was the name of her company," Lee said. "Delia was a critic. She reviewed books for the provincial papers."

Audrey froze, her arms full of books. It was like a gear suddenly clicked into place in her brain. *That's me!* She couldn't believe she had never thought of herself as a critic before.

She realized later, when she scurried outside on her morning break to call Skyla's house on her cell phone, that if she had really wanted to tell Skyla, she would have called the apartment. But she didn't. She called Skyla's house and she felt her heart trip when it was Skyla who picked up.

"Hey," Skyla said flatly.

Audrey opened her mouth, but then pressed it closed again.

"What's up, Audrey?"

She knew Skyla would belittle her discovery; she'd have some small piece of convincing evidence to prove Audrey would never be a good book critic.

"If you're calling to tell me you talked to Emily and Ivy and Josh, I already know." There was a snorting sound. "You'll be glad to know none of them are speaking to me. The summer's been a blast."

On the street, people swished past her.

"Calling me up to chew me out and you can't say a word, can you? Well, guess what, Audrey? I didn't say anything to anybody that you wouldn't have said yourself—"

Audrey shook her head. "I wouldn't say those things." Her voice broke, but she kept going. "I didn't say those things. That's the difference between you and me."

Skyla, quiet as a whisper, said, "And you think that makes you better than me, don't you? I'm so crude and you're so nice and demure and everybody just loves you. Is that what you think? Well, guess what? Thinking what you thought makes you just as crude as me."

Audrey leaned over, there on the sidewalk, one arm wrapped around her waist.

Skyla went on: "I know what you think of me and I know what you think of all our friends. I know what you think of your own mother: You're embarrassed by her." It sounded like Skyla was crying, something Audrey hadn't heard for years. There was a moan and then a pause and then the voice went hard again. "Maybe no one else knows how you think, but I do, so just remember that, Miss Perfect, Miss Refined. I know what you're thinking and you're a foul-mouthed little—"

Audrey hung up. Her hand shook and she felt an incredible heat in her throat; her head buzzed. She couldn't hold it in, and if she tried, she felt like she'd burn from the inside out. She held out the phone and yelled at it, there on the street: "You're a fucking cunt, Skyla Roberts!" She stopped, suddenly aware that bookstore customers walking past had paused. Her voice had been shrill, screeching up and away from her. Lee was at the doorway, staring at her, looking as though she'd tasted something rancid.

Audrey put her hand to her throat. A wash of feelings went through her: She felt ill, but also somehow lighter. Embarrassed, but then – no. Something hardened around that feeling. She flashed, of all things, to Skyla's child-self, swinging her arms wildly while lip-syncing to Madonna, nudging Audrey and giving her that wink, like *You can do this, Audrey. Just watch me.* Barb, leaning forward in her seat, expectant, hopeful.

She smoothed a palm along her pulled-back hair, then walked up the steps past Lee, her back straight. "I'm sorry about that. I had a personal matter to attend to."

Lee hesitated a moment, then gave a slow nod. "In the future—" she began, but Audrey cut her off crisply, even severely:

"*Of course.*"

For about a year after the summer she moved to Victoria, Audrey tried to get in touch with Lesley without going through Skyla, but she never got any emails or phone calls back. Eventually,

Audrey decided Lesley was being loyal to Skyla. Or maybe it was what happened when you moved to the other end of the country. She had lost touch with the others, too, even Josh.

It felt increasingly rude of her mother to bring Skyla up on the phone. "Skyla was by today. She got the part she auditioned for. We're so thrilled! We're taking her to lunch to celebrate tomorrow."

"We?"

"Lesley will come, too. She loved Skyla in that last play. She especially loved the rave reviews!"

Audrey was sitting in her cubicle, a pile of papers in front of her criss-crossed with red-penned comments. "Mother, I really don't have time to chit-chat now," she said. For a moment, she stared at the plastic partitions around her and thought about how silly it was, that if she wanted to she could just kick one over. How flimsy and insubstantial.

"All right, well, don't work too hard, Audrey. Get out and make some friends!"

She caught her reflection in the window across from her desk. *What would we say about me now? Overly ambitious? Bitch? Alone.* She tugged at her fitted jacket and ran her pointing finger over an eyebrow, pressed her red lips together too hard. "What excellent advice, Mother." The last word wobbled.

Her mother was quiet for a moment on the other end, then: "Oh, Audrey, dear…"

Audrey shook her head curtly and hung up the phone.

But that wasn't the worst of it. It was what they both, as girls, would have said about Skyla – *the* Skyla Roberts, up-and-comer. What the reviews said. Audrey had read them, too, of course. She had even clipped one out: *Radiant! Outshines all others. May as well have been the only one on the stage.* Every time she read it, in her mind, the voice was her mother's.

PROGRESSIVE DINNER

Charlotte carried a dish of yams, wrapped in a taut layer of Saran Wrap, under one arm and her fist clutched a paper sack. The dish slipped as she struggled to knock on the front door. She could hear voices from the open front window, but a thin curtain hid faces from view. Shifting the paper bag to her teeth, she poised to knock and heard:

"…seen the way she dresses?"

"Suzy. She'll be here any minute."

"She looks so Toronto. Like, here's my dishevelled expensive scarf and my perfectly straight hair and my PhD in the Philosophy of Education or Grammar, or some such bullshit."

There was a ripping snort of laughter at the exact moment the yam dish slipped to the ground and broke into a collage of ceramic shards and orange lumps at Charlotte's feet.

Suzy continued: "Like I need some kid from down south telling me how to teach English to my students. Management can hire whoever they damn well please."

Whomever, Charlotte thought, allowing her knees to bend, lowering to the front stoop, leaning back on her haunches against the door. Pottery poked at her calf. She tossed it at the withered wild roses.

"Don't take it so personally."

That was Kathleen – not exactly Charlotte's friend, but an amiable colleague she had met a year ago at a conference in

Winnipeg about post-secondary education in Canada's Far North. Charlotte had been there collecting research for her PhD on women in leadership positions in education. Kathleen, all the way from the Yukon, represented Whitehorse's trades college – not the university, but a smaller school, Whitehorse Tech. She was a guidance counsellor of sorts. She recruited kids from the local high school and tried to sell them on higher education. The way she talked about it, Charlotte could tell it was not easy to sell them on higher education at the niche but underfunded school.

Over paper plates of rolled roast beef and cubed cheddar cheese, between two Power Point presentations, they'd fallen into a conversation that ended with Kathleen scrawling her email address on a napkin, saying, "Whitehorse Tech is about to hire a car salesman from Windsor to do the job – you've got to apply. You've got all the right credentials and it would be great to have a woman doing the job."

"I don't have my PhD quite yet," Charlotte had said.

"Maybe we can make an exception if you're the best fit; we've done it before. Our English teacher doesn't even have a master's yet. She's not qualified; she's just the right woman for the job." After the conference, in a burst of optimism, Charlotte had applied for the position.

There was a cranking sound then, and Charlotte realized the front window was being wound open wider.

Kathleen spoke again. "She has a vision for Whitehorse Tech—"

"If I hear the word vision one more time…"

"Suzy, if you're going to smoke in the house, blow it out the window."

Charlotte drew back.

"And that's another thing about our new friend with her PhD. She's got this real thing about smoking."

Charlotte shifted, her butt sticky from yams that had been baked in butter and maple syrup; the bottom of the paper bag rested on her knee, grease bleeding onto her jeans.

"I mean, get over it already," Suzy complained.

Charlotte felt a drop in her stomach, but then realized Suzy meant the smoke – not that Charlotte should or would ever get over her mother dying from lung cancer. No one here knew about her death yet. She hadn't been able to say the words *mother* and *died* or *dead* together. Or even *passed*.

Charlotte looked up from her lap and surveyed the scene from Kathleen's front step. The house was perched in a hilly, quiet subdivision outside of Whitehorse. The front yard was more rock and stone than soil. It held the frosted ghosts of sparse flower beds, a cluster of May trees that looked like they'd already gone to sleep for the winter. From one branch, a clutch of heavy wind chimes sang a forlorn but pretty tune when the wind blew through them.

Charlotte sighed. What Suzy didn't seem to understand, Charlotte thought, is that she had genuinely hoped to help Whitehorse Tech become a better school. She had really believed, at the time she'd taken the position, that breezing in from Toronto fresh with ideas on education, she could whip Whitehorse Tech into a froth. But then her mother had died three weeks before she'd moved up North. Her confidence had gone flaccid, and she'd found herself standing in front of the small staff, talking higher performance expectations with a catch in her throat – Suzy seated in the front row with a stare on her like a pit bull.

Charlotte had grown up in a small town called Briar Bay, on the beaches of Lake Huron, a few hours from Toronto, far enough away to feel rural and detached from the big city and its suburban spill.

Folks in Briar Bay went to Toronto a few times a year for plays and museums and back-to-school shopping. They were farmers and doctors and teachers and artists. They'd chosen Briar Bay because it was not Toronto. But it didn't matter how many times Charlotte told her new colleagues in Whitehorse that she was from Briar Bay, not Toronto – they always asked about the weather or her family back in "the big city." Ontario was all Toronto to them; and Toronto was all bad. And though she liked Toronto, had gone to York, and then to U. of T., Toronto was not her hometown, and she wished people could understand the difference, and what that difference meant to her.

Briar Bay was all violets, lavenders, aquamarine, robin's egg blue, deep lipsticky pinks, and vivid, emerald greens. Charlotte had grown up knowing flower gardens that could not be contained, that grew lusciously with abandon through blazing summers. They popped with yellows, reds, and oranges, sprawling lazily, easily reaching up trellises, bowing over paths that led to familiar front doors.

Here in Whitehorse, Charlotte thought, flower gardens would be encrusted in snow for too many months. She loved Spring, but had been told that the Yukon skipped Spring, going from icy Winter to a dry, dusty Summer almost overnight, sometime around the end of May. She would still be wearing her winter coat come May, Charlotte thought to herself – that swaddling, all-consuming parka Kathleen had lent to her. The first time she had tried it on, Charlotte had felt its weight bearing down on her. Its heaviness impressed on her, for the first time, just how cold it was going to get.

She also loved Autumn – in southern Ontario it lingered for months, firing the hills neon-red and yellow with maples. While here, there had been only the briefest flash of early Autumn colours, a matter of days. By September, the trees had already shed their leaves in yellow-brown heaps, the temperature had plummeted, snow had fallen, melted, and threatened to fall again. The hunched shoulders of Grey Mountain were shrouded white, blending with the expansive, milk-white sky. It was early October and Autumn had passed a month ago, and Winter was there, on the mountains, about to descend upon her.

Last week, she'd been in the college staff room, sipping Folgers with creamer from a Styrofoam cup, trying to look like she felt she should be there. Suzy sat across from her, her big hair teased up at the front, her blue eyes glittering from behind her mug. Charlotte had been talking to Gareth, the college president, trying to find some sliver of connection. He'd spoken in numbers and blamed the college's low enrolment on the local high school. Then he'd switched to talk of Florida, his cats, boating. What had come clear: the college was funded by the government and Gareth wanted more of that funding – he had hired Charlotte to do all the thinking.

Kathleen walked into the staff room. She had worked at the college for 14 years and she really believed that it was a bridge for people in Whitehorse to a better life, as she put it. She was Whitehorse-born and had graduated from the college, and then had gone on to study in Regina, but had moved back home to "give back," she'd told Charlotte.

"Happy Thanksgiving," Kathleen said to Gareth. She turned and smiled at Charlotte. "What are your plans, Charlotte? I take in all the orphans for Thanksgiving dinner every year. I figure I'm already cooking for a crowd – what's a few more? You in?"

Charlotte thought she heard a slight murmur of disapproval from Suzy, but nodded *yes* at Kathleen.

In Briar Bay, Thanksgiving had been shared with three other families in the neighbourhood. Each family took responsibility for a course and the party had moved, course by course, from one house to the next. It was called a "progressive dinner," and the ritual was so comfortable, so familiar that it was nothing for Charlotte to slip in and out of her neighbours' homes, walk through the front doors without even knocking. It wasn't just that her neighbours had known her since she was a baby, but that her sense of belonging was so complete, so unchallenged, she didn't even notice the boundaries anymore, could waltz right in and help herself to a can of pop, rumple the dog's ears, take a seat at the table.

Charlotte had gone home to Briar Bay for Thanksgiving last year; it was just before her mother got sick. Charlotte had just been out on her third date with Peter. Peter, her boyfriend, who was back in Toronto waiting for her, trying hard to understand why he couldn't join her in the Yukon.

That Thanksgiving, when she and Peter had been new, she'd tried to play it cool when she was with her mother. Her mom always asked about boyfriends last, after discussing school and work and friends and politics.

They were in the kitchen, peeling apples – her family was hosting the dessert course for the progressive dinner that year. Charlotte's mom slipped off her jewelry – an oversized onyx ring, her wedding band, several thin silver bangles, and a hammered copper cuff – and clinked them down in a dish, before washing her hands. Charlotte had two older sisters: Grace and Haley. Grace had always idolized their mom – wore weird outfits to school and cut her own bangs – and Haley had been embarrassed by her different-ness at times, but Charlotte just outright *liked* her mom. She smelled spicy, her voice low in the kitchen where they'd peeled apples side by side, listening to Billie Holiday, talking without things coming to a point. Later, they'd found themselves stretched out on the soft couches in the den, watching a Hitchcock movie and drinking herbal tea. They had the same slender fingers and slow, deep-throated laugh. Her mom had asked her, that day, what Charlotte liked about Peter, and that was it. (He's a natural feminist, Charlotte had said. He gets viscerally upset about Conservatives. And he's goofy at the right times, serious at the right times.) And then they had discussed a paper she'd just written on the first generation of female students at Wellesley College and their impact on modern education in the U.S.

Charlotte thought there was no one as lovely, as enticing, as whole as Peter. She liked his voice on the phone (shy, but eager to talk to her), liked that he played rugby (she'd always felt there was something slightly offbeat jockish about the sport) and she liked finding him cocooned in a blanket on his apartment balcony on a cold day, reading Cormac McCarthy, his face turned toward the sun. Sometimes she thought, *You are my magnet*, though she couldn't say this aloud because it sounded silly and dramatic all at once. But it felt this way: an unstoppable draw to him and a click into place as right as a natural force.

So, why hadn't she let him come? Because it was hard to imagine loving him when someone she loved so deeply had been taken away. That's what she'd told him, more or less, a bit at a time, awkward and pained.

Or maybe it was because when someone you love so much dies – like a mother – you can't bear the normalcy of the days following. It feels wrong to brush your teeth in the same bathroom or to hurry to the same bus stop and laugh at your boyfriend's jokes. Like normal. You have to get away from the shell of normal because nothing interior feels normal at all – Charlotte believed (and also knew it to be unreasonable to believe) that everything should have changed when her mother died; the world itself should have changed.

But, at a certain point after one's mother dies, Charlotte was learning, people who care for you begin saying the words "moving on" or "moving forward" – and Charlotte did not like these words. Her body got tight around the innermost part of her self, the part where she stored the sensation of still having a mother, of having *her* mother. And having her mother was something she had felt like its own little heart inside of her, a heart that now seemed at risk of dissolving into a nothingness that physically hurt.

She found it easier to be in a place where her mother had never been, easier to not imagine bringing Peter home to Briar Bay, to not imagine marrying him in the garden among her mom's poppies, to not imagine having a baby, holding the baby on her lap and drinking coffee in the morning at the oak table with Peter and her sisters in the house where her mother would never be. She could not, would not, experience that kitchen if it did not have the smell of her mother glazing the very texture of the air.

The more people Charlotte met in the Yukon, the more she thought most people who had moved here had come here to be away from something. There were many kilometres of the rocky, ice-cloaked mountain range to separate one from whatever might need getting away from. When she'd flown into White-horse for the first time, she'd felt the lonely, relieving sensation that she was landing on the moon. Now she felt that perhaps too many people had stayed here too long on their moon – they conveyed a certain determined shut out of the rest of the world. They called the rest of the world *Outside*, as in, "This is Charlotte. She's from Outside." As though where she was from did not deserve a close look, could be lumped in with anywhere else.

Still, she was curious about this northern town. She felt, in some way, that it was important for her to be there. She had never been this far north – and she soon realized that she had never even imagined what it was like to be this far north. This made her feel both arrogant and incredibly isolated – she lived in a place that was easy to not even think about.

Then there was the dream. It came to her at least once a week: she and her mother are standing by an impervious, dark grey rock face. None of the gentle rainbow easiness of home. Her mother keeps reaching into her pockets, pulling out fistfuls of seeds, which she flings at the rock wall, over and over, encouraging Charlotte to do the same, and Charlotte thinks, *Flowers won't grow here, Mom*, and her mother says to her, *Yes, they will, Char. Throw.* Looking at the rock face in her dream, she watches the seeds explode into tiny beads of paint, transforming the greyness into fuchsia and mauveine and cerulean and citrine.

On Kathleen's front step, the coldness of the cement bled through Charlotte's jeans, spreading a chill through her body. Since Charlotte had moved to Whitehorse, Kathleen had taken her under her wing. Not just siding with her at staff meetings, but also sitting with her in the cafeteria, inviting her over for Sunday dinners – even though Charlotte sensed that things at home were not as easy for Kathleen as she liked to let on. She had four kids, including Bella who had some kind of behavioural disorder that no one talked about, and a husband who seemed uninterested in conversations about the college, but Kathleen always served something hot and cheesy to keep the children full and entertained, and she made up for her husband's recalcitrance by having plenty of her own talk. And so, Charlotte felt all right with her.

Which was not as good as feeling loved, or feeling that she belonged, as she did at the progressive dinners, seated between people she had ridden with on the school buses, swum with in the lake. They knew her parents – her mother, the artist who smoked clove cigarettes, her dad, bearded, a bit of a nerd. They knew Charlotte's shyness for what it was and did not mistake it for snobbishness.

For the progressive dinners, her mother wore a dress – something bohemian, she liked vintage and dark red. She wouldn't change into the dress until after the cooking was done. She moved fluidly around the kitchen, her long hair up in a loose bun, chopping onions or rolling pastry dough, calling out requests to her daughters: "Charlotte, can you light the candles? Use the wooden holders. Add a cushion to that chair for Arnie." She was calm, at ease in the moments before guests arrived. She was almost always in a semi-dreamy state, though she never missed a detail; her gaze soft; her focus sharp. Charlotte's dad would get messy and a bit flustered, and her mother would swipe cranberry from his arm and flick off the burner he'd left on and then swing by the cabinet to select a Nina Simone CD for when friends arrived.

Over Grey Mountain, a disc of cloud grew heavier and Charlotte thought she smelled snow. Charlotte stared hard at the bluish-grey of the mountain and tried to place the exact shade, to match it with one of the tubes of paint in her mother's many drawers and boxes. Her mom had taken over the sun porch back home. She had covered the floor with rugs and kept a pile of afghans and quilts that she'd drape over her lap when she painted in the colder months. Sometimes Charlotte wandered inside when her mother wasn't home and she'd touch the canvases and finger the tubes of paint and wooden stems of paintbrushes. She'd find half-drunk cups of tea in handcrafted pottery on the dresser or on the floor and she'd smell her mother's clove cigarettes mixed with the chemical, acrid scent of paint and the clear, cold air leaking in from outside. She'd pause to study the colour wheel thumb-tacked to the wall, or press a flake of gold leaf into the pad of her finger and snail-trail it up her arm.

Always, she stared into her mother's landscapes, wondering about this world her mother melted into where she could sit in front a blank swath of canvas and, stroke after stroke, layer of colour upon layer of colour, create a place where there had been only white, a blank.

The mountains were slate grey today, Charlotte thought, or perhaps cadet. The sparse trees were thin as toothpicks, giving her a poetic feeling, and the sky had a soft, pearly sheen. Everywhere she looked, she was reminded that her mother could no longer be seen or smelled or heard.

"Maybe she's not coming," Kathleen said, her voice clear, as though she had stepped closer to the window.

"You and your stray cats," Suzy said. "Honestly, any minute she could decide you need a higher certification to stay at your own job." A stream of cigarette smoke snaked its way past Charlotte.

"She only recommended to management that we start thinking about higher credentials. Nothing's been decided yet and no one's being fired. She's just here to observe and give ideas."

"Here's an observation: the rules are different up here—"

"Oh, dammit!" Kathleen said suddenly. "This is exactly what I worried would happen. I've ended up feeding her to the lions. I honestly thought, when I met her at that conference in Winnipeg, that bringing in someone from the Outside would be a breath of fresh air, that we'd all benefit from it. We've gotten so complacent at the college. I hate to speak against Gareth, but he's just driving us into the ground. We barely get some of these kids from the high school and then we do so little for them."

"Kath—"

Kathleen kept going. "We're not doing them justice, letting the college slide like this. If they want to go elsewhere to study, that's fine, but I don't want Whitehorse Tech to be their last resort. I want them to be excited about it. Like what I see in Charlotte when she talks about education. Or what I saw. Her whole body would light up. You should see Bella, Suzy, when she comes home from school. There's no air in her at all. It's like she's been staring at blank walls all day."

"Kathleen." There was a pause. "Your kids are going to be fine. Bella will be fine. You don't have to go anywhere else to have a good higher education. We're in a slump, that's all. Gareth needs to pull up his socks. What our students need is a president who's as passionate about the college as you are."

"But until we get that, are the kids going to do okay?"

"They do okay. Even in the fancy universities, some of the kids love learning and some of them don't."

There was a long, quiet moment. Charlotte sat very still, head cocked, sensitive to the silence. She remembered something her mother used to do – brush a wash of watercolour over oils to change the tint. *Why do you do that?* Charlotte had asked. *To see differently*, her mom had said. She felt her skin go prickly with a flush of arrogance. She'd been looking at it all wrong. Perhaps provincialism had its useful side – a person who loved it here, who loved it as much as she loved Briar Bay – would be in a better position to invigorate the school. What they needed was someone who knew the students like they knew their own sons and daughters. It was a different world, and progressive as Charlotte hoped her ideas were, she was beginning to understand that, here, her education was incomplete.

Then Suzy spoke: "Actually, Kath," she cleared her throat. "I've kind of been thinking about going back to school. Not because that's what Charlotte recommended…"

"Suzy," Kathleen said. "That's wonderful. A really wonderful idea. And Charlotte never said you had to—"

"For a year or two. I'd come back—"

"No, I know. You should go, Suzy. You should do it."

"Sometimes I feel like, I don't know… I don't know—"

"Really, you do just fine—"

"No, I don't mean about English or teaching."

Charlotte remembered her mother, fastening her earrings in the moments before a progressive dinner would begin, taking the time to put on her favourite red lipstick – *crushed merlot*, Charlotte recalled – before the neighbours arrived.

She could almost feel her mother then, kneeling beside her, then standing, that calm force she exuded, like she could always see through the tangible world into a layer beneath. She had a way of blurring the surface. Charlotte stood and breathed sharply through her nose and knocked on the door.

"Oh, thank goodness," she heard Kathleen say, and then a moment later she was opening the door, Suzy behind her, and without her usual frown. Kathleen said: "Charlotte. We were just beginning to worry."

Charlotte paused, hesitating on the doorstep. She felt something inside her beginning to unwind, but it was not so sorrowful a sensation as it had been before.

Then Suzy stepped toward her and offered to take her coat. "Can I look after that for you?" she said.

Charlotte felt a strange unravelling. She began unpeeling her scarf. She was nodding. It was unspooling, just loop after loop slipping to the floor, but she nodded, sensing that at the end of all that unravelling there would still be something – if paler or changed – at the core of it. She decided she would wait until after the dinner to call Peter and tell him she that was coming home.

"Yes," she said, and stepped inside.

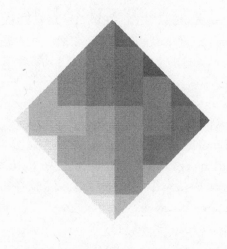

THE FLY SWIMMER

Sonia was in the passenger seat, her body a tight twist turned toward the back. Her son was gagging on a cough drop he'd excavated from a crevice in the back of the car.

"Got it, we're good, I'm pulling over." Bert was calm, one eye on his son in the rear-view mirror. "He's not purple; that's good."

"Jesse, keep coughing," Sonia coached. "I can't tell if he's choking or not," she yelped.

Jesse made a wheezing sound followed by a wet hack.

"If you can hear them coughing, it's good. I think I heard that somewhere." Bert was easing the car to the shoulder. "Okay, almost there. We're good."

"Stop saying it's good! This is not good. Jesse, keep coughing." The car came to a halt, and Sonia catapulted into the back seat at the exact moment a ruby lozenge flew from Jesse's mouth. It hit the back of the passenger's seat with a sticky tap. Jesse gurgled, gasped, then pitched a one-note wail.

"It's okay, honey, it's okay. I've got you, I'm here." Sonia pinched open the car seat buckles, wrenched him onto her lap. "No problem. See? You're fine, now."

Bert got out and opened the back door, leaned in. "Hey, Champ. Well done. Both of you." He winked at his wife.

Sonia turned her face from him and pressed her nose into Jesse's sweet, sweaty hair smell. She couldn't even rely on Bert to panic, she thought to herself.

Fifteen kilometers later, Sonia slipped into a half-sleep, her arm tacky against the black plastic of Jesse's car seat. He was asleep.

Roused, she levered one leg forward, then the next, into the front, rotating her hips and settling cross-legged. Years of yoga with Diana had given her a body that could perform hairpin turns and slide itself through needle-eye openings. She turned to Bert: "That was scary."

"Ah, no big deal. I choke like that all the time. I eat too fast. But I can't help it. Sometimes food is just so good. You know?"

A memory that had been packed away long ago returned to her in faded colour: smoking pot together in the dark in the high school soccer field and how the taste of a single orange Skittle had blown her mind.

Bert smiled that smile at her, the one where he was trying to make her feel better and not totally sure which tact to take. He said, "Do you need anything? I think all your stuff's at your feet."

A cloth bag on the floor held lavender essential oil, an aromatherapy spritz named Calling All Angels, and several small glass vials of herbal tinctures. These had been prescribed to her by Diana, her naturopathic doctor-cum-yoga instructor. There was also a book that Diana had recommended: *Taming the Beast*. Pressed like a flower between its pages was a list of wellness goals Sonia had been working on throughout the long cross-country car ride from Vancouver to southwestern Ontario. The first was "Stop freaking out," (Diana had gently reprimanded her for this – it wasn't kindly stated self-talk). The second was "Just keep swimming" a line borrowed from Jesse's favourite Disney movie that sometimes stopped a cork in a mild panic attack.

She reached in her bag for the spritz and misted the back seat, then turned the bottle on herself, breathing in as deeply as she could. She was aware that her deep breathing these days was not all that deep – that her *ujjayi*, or ocean breath in yoga class, lasted a full five seconds less than Diana's luxurious inhales and exhales which sounded, indeed, as mystic and unphased as the ocean itself. Her own breath was a dry wind sucked through a fissure.

She tucked the spray away, not bothering to offer any to Bert, who eyed her growing collection of vials and teas with a bemused wariness.

They were nearing Clifford, she knew without checking the map. She hadn't lived here since she was a child, but the feel of the place was deeply familiar, which surprised her. She had prepared to be disappointed by a reality that wouldn't live up to her memories of idyllic farmland and the glorious lake. But here, lazy cows with liquid eyes swung their heads and slapped their tails against their haunches, as though in a cartoon. The fields were freshly ploughed under, revealing soil as moist and rich as dark chocolate cake.

Occasionally, they passed yellow-bricked farmhouses, sun-bleached yet sturdy, looking so sure of themselves; after all, they'd survived trees split and spit onto their roofs in wild thunderstorms, survived rasping, thrashing blizzards. They were so much more magnificent than the slippery, translucent condos of Vancouver.

In front of one farmhouse, children sloshed around a slip-n-slide, hair glossy against their heads, gleaming like otters. Their shrieks swirled through Sonia's open window. A little girl in a lavender polka-dotted bathing suit watched Sonia as the car glided past, and languidly, sweetly lifted a middle finger. Sonia pressed back into her seat and stared straight ahead at the country road, startled, and for some reason, comforted.

Then they rose up a gentle hill; both Sonia and Bert breathed in sharply. The glittering blue of Lake Huron lay before them as far as they could see and beyond, water forever, and Bert said something about it being an ocean. Sonia couldn't speak; it was so beautiful she felt her body had gone liquid.

"The Freshwater Sea," she said, the name coming back to her from some other time and place.

Jesse was still asleep when they reached Hayes Road on the outskirts of Clifford. Bert was trying to remember where he had put the directions to their rental house. Sonia rifled through the glove box, and with a ripple of irritation found the note pressed into a Ziploc bag with folding papers and loose bud. After 12 years together, she should have known better than to expect Bert to keep important things such as directions in a logical place. She uncreased the note, ignoring its new smell, and said, "We're going to pass right by the Forest Schoolhouse. Do you want to stop?"

The schoolhouse was the whole reason for moving back to Ontario. Or it was the explicable part of the whole reason.

One day about a year ago, when Sonia had been off work, battling an impending anxiety attack, she'd found herself trawling the internet, looking for some place to settle – she wasn't quite sure where. She'd been doing this since Jesse's birth, looking for a house or a town, or maybe a group of people who might make her feel better. She didn't know why exactly, but she felt a new geography was necessary. Vancouver was no longer the leafy, quiet, romantic place it had been for her in her teens and early 20s – the pretty city had an ego now. Sonia felt this ego announce itself to her every time she stepped into a bakery to buy bread or coffee with Jesse on her hip. She would step up to the counter and feel unqualified to make the order. Should she speak French? Was it completely forbidden to ask for decaf? It was impossible to know how much anything cost because the handwritten chalking was always too European a script to decipher. If Jesse squawked out "Cookie!" she was relieved and left it at that.

She and Bert had often talked about moving somewhere entirely different once they were able to afford it (and they could now, thanks to an investment her parents had made in her name). Peru! Barcelona, or later New York, then Maine, Quebec. She kept circling Ontario, knowing Bert had no draw whatsoever to that province. But she did. She missed those farms and the concession roads, the little towns with oddball names: Dorking, Bervie, Dornoch. She missed the blindingly sunny summers, the dry tingling just before the skin seared on your nose. She wanted to swim in the humidity, feel the eruptive roar of the winds off Lake Huron, and be back in a place she had been herself long before she'd ever become Bert's girlfriend, then wife. Or, perhaps all mothers who loved their childhoods want to take their own children back to them, to those years, those places, that peaceable kingdom.

So she'd sat at her computer that day, in their tight, bright condo of all-white surfaces, seeking. A timer on her laptop went *pi-ping*, reminding her to meditate. Just as she was about to go to her room (the meditation broom closet, Bert called it, for that's what it had once been) a posting caught her eye: *The Clifford Forest Schoolhouse*, someone had written on a thread on a self-help blog, *is inspired by alternative education systems, such as Waldorf and Montessori, but we do not adhere to one philosophy other than the belief in respecting childhood and our natural environment.*

Clifford Forest Schoolhouse was a hotlink. Sonia clicked and was taken to a website with a picture of a cottage-schoolhouse surrounded by a wild, rainbow-coloured growth of flowers and vegetables. A stone path led to the front door and curled from one side. Out front, as though growing from the tall grass, was a cob oven tended by a long-haired man in a grey apron. Other people flanked the school: a woman with corkscrew curls in an ankle-length orange skirt, a bespectacled man with a newsboy cap. They sported big, organic smiles, flushed cheeks, mussed hair, bold colours in cloths that Sonia just *knew* were natural fabrics.

On the steps sat some students: a cluster of kids held some kind of knitted craft in their hands. Behind them stood a lean, muscular woman with white-blonde hair in a soft-looking grey T-shirt and beautifully faded jeans. Her smile was wide and bleach-white. Sonia could tell from the cut of her shirt that it was expensive. (Later, Bert and Diana would refer to this website scene as Sonia's "J. Crew catalogue fantasy school," but Sonia would never know that.) To Sonia, it seemed more than just a fancy school for privileged kids. These were exactly the people she wanted for Jesse.

The more she read, the more enchanted she became until, by the time Bert had come home from work, she was imagining walking Jesse to the front step of the school on a morning cut from golden silk, pausing to exchange zucchini bread recipes with the the blonde-haired woman. She envisioned herself in a cornflower blue sundress, Birkenstocks – the sleek kind. In her enthusiasm, the anxiety attack had shrunk to the size of a plum, then a pea, then a pebble, until she could slough it aside with the back of her hand. She'd taken this as a good omen. At the moment, she was into omens. Diana had told her that the universe speaks in signs.

"This is exactly the place I've been imagining for you and for me and Jesse. Just look at these people. And Bert, it's only, like, ten kilometres from where I lived before my family moved west. I think this is it."

Bert could be tumbleweed, easy to roll, but still, it took a while before he was fully convinced. It was not that he was loyal to his job or Vancouver or even their friends, but to something Sonia could not get him to name.

When they got out of the car in Clifford, Sonia smelled baked, mineral-rich dirt, dried corn husks, and the tang of the fresh-water sea – not saltwater, but a clean, fishy scent that washed her hair back from her face, made her skin feel softer. While Vancouver had morphed into an ultra-trendy, hipsterish super-city, Clifford had stayed still. No. It had done better; it had gone both back in time and into a progressive future, erecting a schoolhouse where the beautiful children of kindly, organic farmers and bakers learned to raise bees and knit their own socks.

Bert was at a window of the schoolhouse, pressing his face to it, hands cupped on either side of his eyes. "Looks great, Babe," he called to her. "I think Jesse is going to like it." They passed the cob oven, tucking their heads as though they were country-wise to ovens, and admired a two-storey tree house that had a rope ladder, a periscope, and a flag that read, "Forest World," the letters painted by children. They were inspecting a circle of wooden toadstools big enough for grown-ups to sit on, when the sunset's colours hijacked the sky. Blazing pink and orange and purple soared up from the water's glinting sapphire and the last slice of glowing sun melted over the horizon. Sonia put a hand on her chest and felt a wave swelling.

Diana had warned Sonia that wherever she went, her anxiety would follow. It was not a matter of outrunning it, she had said, but rather of befriending it. Sonia didn't often doubt Diana. It felt good to have complete faith in a person. But maybe, Sonia thought, we are all given this one lone place where we feel good, where bad things can't follow. Maybe this rural town in south-western Ontario was some kind of parallel universe for her. Perhaps her pre-anxiety self had been left here and could be reclaimed; there could be a reacquaintance.

Over the years, Diana had asked a lot of questions about her marriage and she had urged Sonia to make decisions independent of Bert's needs. Sonia, sitting opposite Diana, thought how much her naturopathic doctor had tried to help her, how every herbal remedy and meditation technique and yoga posture that she recommended had made Sonia feel she should be getting better. "Healing is a journey," Diana had said.

Sonia had been feeding Bert bits and pieces of Diana's advice for years. And, as the connection between Sonia and her husband had begun to erode, she suggested that Bert talk to Diana himself. "You don't have to talk to her about *him*," she said, knowing Bert would slip from her, like a turtle sliding into its shell, if she suggested talking about his father. "Just talk to her about us."

Bert had looked confused. "What does *naturopathic* mean again? I thought she was like a doctor, only with herbs."

"The mind and the body are inextricable," Sonia said, annoyed that she had to keep explaining Diana.

For so long, Sonia had felt secure inside herself. Then she began feeling little cracks in that security, and panic overtook her, rising up and swelling so painfully against her breastbone that she felt she had to release it, all at once, explosively. But that seemed wrong, destructive. Especially once Jesse arrived. All the anger she'd been nurturing, carefully tending to, felt juvenile when she held infant Jesse close, his creamy skin and the soft rise of his chest reminding her of a too easily forgotten delicateness. So the anger shifted inside her, curled up, a dragon with its snout to its tail.

It became a kind of fear instead – fear of dropping one of the mundane details of her life, or peeling back an element – employment, marriage, location – and seeing that it was all veneer. Becoming a mother, for Sonia, had drawn a very clear, un-erasable line between that which was solid and true in her life, and that which was flimsy. She wanted a brick farmhouse; she feared she lived in one of those magic-trick homes you see in *National Geographic* – a thatched roof settled on walls of woven grass, on *stilts*, propped in a turbulent ocean, relying on a logic she couldn't grasp. But what was it, exactly? Sonia wondered.

What in her life was she trying to balance on such an impossible foundation?

"Perhaps it's Bert," Diana said in her bare-boned way. It was amazing how she could do that, Sonia thought. She could speak such harsh truths, seemingly without judgment or motive, so that there was no cause for offence. But no, Sonia protested. That's too easy, a woman blaming her husband for her unhappiness mid-marriage. Diana lifted one of her shapely brows. She knew their entire history – Sonia had spent many of their one-hour-long appointments talking out their backstory, how Bert had started smoking too much pot, then jumped from urban farmer to failed entrepreneur to landscaper. Then there was an accident: they were having sex one night and Bert, stoned, said "For sure" when Sonia asked, "Did you get the condom on properly?" and then they were pregnant.

Worse, even though they'd promised each other they would not have children – even though it had been Bert who'd said he just couldn't do it, would be so freaked out if it ever happened – when the pregnancy test showed positive he had pressed her against him in an all-consuming hug, saying, "This is really, really good." When he had released her, Sonia went into the bathroom, locked the door and laid her head on the cooling tile.

She had thought deciding not to have children was a great sacrifice she had made for Bert. How noble that sacrifice made her feel. But she'd known a truth in that moment on the bathroom floor: the idea of a having a child was both something she painfully wanted and something she could not imagine possible with Bert. How could he do it? He sometimes forgot to brush his own teeth. She would kick at him in bed. "Bert, I can smell your teeth." "Oh. Oh yeah, totally forgot." He would get up and go to the bathroom and pee, and come back to bed still not having brushed. She was keeping him afloat. She could feel that.

"There's a thin skin between normal adult functionality and some kind of disintegration for Bert," Sonia told Diana during one of their sessions. Pot seemed like his best idea for normalcy; Sonia thought perhaps it skewed his idea of normal, made certain things, old pain, tolerable to him, but other things, mundane things, unreachable, meaningless. Her best sense of normalcy for Bert was herself. As long as she was attached to him, he'd be okay. He'd get up for work, and celebrate Thanksgiving and unload the dishwasher. Most of the time. Diana took a sip of her tea, when Sonia told her this, and said nothing.

At the schoolhouse, they leaned against the hood of the car and watched the reds of the sunsets darken into purples and the purples into blues. Bert rolled a joint. As always, he offered it to Sonia and, as always, she said, "No, thank you."

He knew to respond: "I'm cutting back in Ontario. Just twice a day."

The heat and the cricket song and the sunset had softened her edges. "It's not really a problem unless you're really stoned."

He looked at her, sadness around his eyes. "I'll do my best," he said.

Bert had been Albert Jr., then just Albert, then Bert. He showed up in Sonia's homeroom in Grade Nine. He came through the door, lanky, light freckles and sandy hair and sad-looking grey eyes, and she had had two reactions to him at once: she wanted him and she wanted to reassure him. She had never felt a strong sexual attraction to anyone before. She followed the feeling through its vortex, and was still there.

He looked down and then went to the seat the teacher pointed him to without glancing around. She thought he seemed much older than 15 – not in looks, but in the way he sat, wearily, as though he'd been walking for days. She stared at the back of him for the rest of the class, thinking that the back of his neck was better looking than the face of any boy at school.

Because of his good looks and his loping grace on the basketball court, Albert Jr. did not take long to adjust to his new Vancouver high school. Luckily for him, he arrived in time for try-outs, and pretty soon most of the guys liked him because he played quite well but never showed off, and all the girls grew crushes on him because he was new and cute. By Christmas, most of the girls had moved on to someone else, but Sonia kept her eyes on the back of his neck and prepared herself for the day he'd turn around.

It happened in February. The homeroom teacher had moved the desks around the day before and when they'd entered in the morning he pointed out where he wanted them all to sit. They were starting a unit on algorithms and he was going to ask them to work in pairs. "Get to know your partner. Lean on each other."

She'd been distracted by a discovery made in swim practice that morning: She could outswim the team captain in the butterfly. It was one of the delicious victories of her high school career. Her triceps still tingled. The feeling of propelling her body through the cold pool water coursed through her and made her want to paddle at the air with cupped palms, pull it strongly around her, to keep surging forward.

Her ponytail was wet and dripping onto the back of her swim team sweatshirt. She was wearing a jean skirt and had forgotten tights so was going to have to call her mom for a ride. All of this was on her mind when the teacher called her name and pointed to a seat. She slid into her new chair, releasing her binder which she'd been hugging to her chest. When she looked up, it was him. The freckles and the hollow sea-grey eyes. Neither of them said a word. Just looked at each other. Brad Phelps walked by and pressed her wet ponytail into the back of her neck. "Nice legs, McGuire."

"Keep your eyes on the road, Phelps," she shot back. A few boys snickered and Brad looked mildly embarrassed, but recovered nicely. She turned back to Bert and he raised one eyebrow. She felt the sensation she'd had earlier that morning, of lifting her body from the water into the air.

A couple of weeks later, Bert asked her how to do a particularly difficult problem and she knew the answer. A big exam was scheduled and he asked if she'd help him study.

"I never see you at the basketball games," he said, after they'd settled in the cafeteria with their textbooks and two Seven-ups.

She was surprised at his non-math related words. "I'm on the swim team," she blurted. "Actually, I was just made fly swimmer."

"Oh," was all he said.

"On the medley team," she went on. "It means I swim the butterfly leg; it's the hardest leg." *Oh, shut up*, she added to herself.

He dug a pencil out from his school bag.

"I mean the butterfly stroke is largely considered the most difficult stroke." She closed her eyes and turned her head away, aghast at herself. Had she really just said the word *stroke* to him, twice?

Two girls walked by, eyes drawn to him until the moment he might have seen them, but then they looked purposefully away, laughing at nothing. Sonia swallowed. She could feel her chance slipping away.

"I never see you at the swim competitions." She said this out of desperation, but it came out in a surprisingly flirty cadence she wasn't used to hearing in her voice. She hid her astonishment at herself.

He studied her. "Then you're not looking," he said.

That was it, for her.

The rental house in Clifford was really a cottage, up a hill from the lake. It had a Seventies feel, though the owners had taken pains to modernize it – vivid blue-green paint, laminate wood flooring, IKEA furniture. Evening light filtered through oak leaves, patterning a dappled, underwater effect on the front lawn. They could hear the soft fumble of waves.

Bert carried a sleepy Jesse inside and laid him down in the only bedroom. Bert had done the lion's share of driving across the country. She'd offered, but he'd said he liked being in "the zone" (pot, Band of Horses, and a Ziploc bag of sunflower seeds).

He dug out a blanket from the trunk of the car and dragged it to the couch.

"Come sleep with me," Sonia said. She had found a pullout sofa on the screened-in porch. Through the trees, she could make out the darkened blues of the lake merging into the night sky.

Surprised, Bert walked wordlessly onto the porch and flapped out the blanket. Sonia laid back. She felt like a kid on summer vacation. The house smelled like the cabin she'd stayed in at summer camp – moldy, minerally, and like sunscreen. "Isn't this awesome?" she whispered, turning to Bert, but he had fallen asleep. He smelled like weed and French fries.

Shortly after they started going out, she introduced him to the high school's pool and taught him to swim, and in the water his body relaxed and moved with natural ease.

"You're good at this!" she yelled to him from the deep end of the pool as he practiced the front crawl.

He breaststroked toward her, wet and shining, a lightness in his eyes. "You think so?"

"Yeah! I think maybe your basketball training helps. Makes you super-smooth."

He laughed. It was an off-kilter laugh. "My dad says I'm not natural at anything. He says I'm like an alien put down on Earth from another planet. I can't do anything right here." He pulled away then and she had watched him and realized, oh, that's the hollowness. That's how come he moves like a wounded man all the time. For some reason – perhaps for no other reason than she wanted to believe it – her next thought was, *I can help him.*

"Show me the butterfly," he called suddenly from the other side of the pool.

She hesitated for a moment, then kicked off the wall full throttle, ducked her head down into the water like a seal, then up with gravity-defying will, pure might, kiss the sky, spine arched to pierce the water, and then – *BOOM*, legs slapping down like a whale's tail, arms caressing the water along the sides, flicking back, emerging as wings, that upward stroke again, up, up.

When she glided to a stop in front of him, and raised her eyes, water dripping down her face, the overhead fluorescent lights bouncing off her, he was beaming, his eyes sparking at her. "Fuck yeah," he whispered.

By Grade 11, Bert and Sonia had been dating for two years. They were a given in high school. They walked the halls together and ate sandwiches in the cafeteria and made no big show of being in love. At the beginning, there was a calmness to it. A solidity. Occasionally, other girls tried to flirt their way between them, but Bert was not interested. He didn't make a lot of other friends. Just a few buddies from the team that were minimal talkers like himself. But he was the kind of quiet that draws people in, so it seemed like he was always near the centre of a crowd.

He started smoking and showed up at school with a black eye. The guidance counselor, Mr. Sendak, made a habit of bumping into him, but couldn't get Bert to actually come into his office.

Sometimes they'd be at Sonia's house, having had dinner with her family, sitting on the swings in the backyard, linking their feet, and she'd sense something bad had happened to him. But he never said anything she could get hold of, just, "My dad won't let me out this weekend."

Increasingly, Bert's dad had work for his son to do – digging a sewage trench, cutting down trees – hard labour that kept him from getting out in the evenings or on weekends. Sonia was never invited to his house. "Pretty dingy," was all he said.

When he showed up at school with scrapes on his arms, he told people it was from a slip on the shingles. Sonia didn't ask; she watched, nodding along, assuring anyone listening that she had been there, too; that this is what had happened. But there was something in his eyes – a quick dart toward her after the story had worked, not a wink, but almost like it. It's our secret now, he seemed to say. But it wasn't, really. Sonia didn't know what secret she was keeping.

"Are you—"

"Fucking *don't*, Sone." He had never talked like that to her before and she flushed.

In her mind she said, *You'd tell me if something was really wrong, right?* And in her mind, he answered, *Yeah, sure.* Somehow, she left it at that. They were going to graduate, and move in together close to UBC. He wasn't planning on university, but she was on track and had worked out the finances with her parents. A couple more years of dealing with his dad and they'd never have to cope with him again.

Shortly after the black eye, Bert, without calling Sonia, missed a week of school. The guidance counselor, Mr. Sendak, summoned her to his office and shut the door.

"How's the swim team, Captain?"

"Great." Mr. Sendak was well-liked by the students, but Sonia had not been in his office before and the seriousness of Bert's absence suddenly hit her. She felt her face go bloodless.

"You okay, Sonia?"

"Yeah. Yep." But it was a struggle to breathe. "Sorry… I'm not sure – I don't feel right."

"Take slow, deep breaths, Sonia. You're okay. Come have a seat on the floor." He helped ease her down to the ground and put a hand on her shoulder and breathed with her, demonstrating a long, slow exhale. "You're okay. You're doing great."

It passed. It suddenly occurred to her: she was sitting on the floor with her guidance counselor. But she didn't want to get up. She wanted to know if Bert was all right.

Mr. Sendak was quiet for a moment. "I think you just had a mild panic attack. These happen. Remember, if it happens, to breathe slowly. In and out, not just in. And get down low to the ground in case you need to pass out. Don't go off alone if you feel that way."

He waited for her to acknowledge this and then went on.

"Bert's in the hospital. He's doing all right, but he was hurt pretty badly. He said he was fixing a window and fell from the second storey and cracked his ribs—"

Sonia found herself shaking her head no.

Mr. Sendak waited with a patience Sonia felt. It came from a place of deep care and kindness. She leaned into it. On his desk was a picture of a woman, 30-something, elfish-looking, with short black hair, a wildness about her eyes. There was some story about his wife having overdosed a decade ago, before he'd come to this school. All of a sudden the possible truth of this high school rumour was like a pin pushed into Sonia's heart and she felt her body curl inward involuntarily.

Still, Mr. Sendak waited. The quietness between them widened and softened and at one point was just the right size and shape for her to speak into, but in the next second she lost her nerve, yet again. "What do you know, Sonia?" His voice was serious, no-nonsense, but also so sad, Sonia thought. She realized that he genuinely hurt when his students hurt. This was compassion.

"I don't know anything."

"What do you know about Bert's home life?"

"I have no idea," she said, the truth of this suddenly astonishing and embarrassing her. *Bert*, she thought, *you're a master criminal. You leave no tracks. Nothing to report on.*

Mr. Sendak smiled, but it was the kind of smile that made her feel bad. "Okay." He helped her up from the floor. "I respect that." He stood with her for a moment before opening his door. She could feel him scrolling her mind as he held the door for her, still the faint, sad smile. She was almost through when he said as though he didn't want to: "Sonia, just one thing: you can't sustain this. You need to know that. In the end, you just can't."

A few days after their arrival in Ontario, there was an open invitation to the Clifford community to pitch in at a working bee for the schoolhouse. Sonia, having read about this on their website, had timed it just so; she wanted to make a good impression on the staff and other parents, and what better way than to show up ready to fix a broken step on the tree house ladder?

She baked ginger snaps, rifling around in the half-unpacked boxes for measuring spoons and baking soda, changed her outfit three times, then stood at the mirror with a tube of mascara in her fingers for a few minutes, then dropped it back into the drawer. She walked down the hall, then back, and applied a light coat to her lashes. When it was time to go, she called for Bert and Jesse but got no answer. They had been talking about the beach before, so she put the cookies in the car and walked to the top of the hill.

It was a cool, late August morning and there were only a few swimmers dipping and resurfacing sleekly, like some kind of marine animals native only to Lake Huron. She spotted Jesse, his pants getting wet in the surf, and Bert beside him, smoking a joint. She watched them for a moment through the leaves of the birch trees. Bert had fallen easily in love with Jesse, they both had, and most of the time, she was surprised to find she didn't feel the damage of Bert's father tainting Bert's own growth into fatherhood. It was just all the pot. The constant urge to escape from his thoughts, or whatever it was that weed now did for him. Sometimes she worried it would make him unsafe with Jesse. He'd miss one of those minute details you suddenly become attuned to as a parent – a hole in the yard fence when your toddler's just begun to run, an uncovered electrical outlet, water boiling on the front burner of the stove. She kept waiting for Bert to misstep. Watching for it made her skin tight. But he hadn't yet.

When they had all settled in the car, she turned to him: "It's really important that they like us, Bert."

He gave her a foggy look. "You mean for Jesse, right?"

She was busy wiping the sand from Jesse's face. She put his tweed cap back on his head, and he pulled it off.

"Okay, Mommy'll hold it for now," she said.

Then to Bert: "It would have been better if you hadn't smoked. Now it's all up to me." She was irritated to find that she was also somewhat relieved – sober Bert could be too aloof with strangers.

When they arrived, she gathered up the cookies and took a deep breath and walked toward a small cluster of women. She had hoped Jesse would stick close to her, he made her feel calm, but he went running for the swings and Bert loped behind him. In moments, Jesse had climbed up onto a double-seater with a girl his age and Bert was leaning against the swing-set talking to a man in a straw hat.

"Welcome!" a woman said to Sonia from the cluster. "Have you come to help out?"

Sonia swallowed.

The woman smiled. "Well, come on in. We're just taking a short break. We've been picking what we can from the garden. It's always a mess when we get back to it in August. I'm Marla. I teach kindergarten. Meet Ebony, Raya, and Claire."

Each woman smiled at Sonia and stuck out a hand. When she got to Claire, Sonia recognized her as the woman in the photo, and muttered, "Oh!" which she then tried to cover up by coughing, as Claire's eyes widened. In person, she was even more attractive, her skin luminescent and taut, her bright eyes taking Sonia in.

Sonia ventured: "I'm Sonia and we're new here, my husband and son and I. From Vancouver. We love the Forest School," she added and then wished she could take it back because it sounded gushy.

"Oh, I hope you didn't move all the way out here just for the school," Claire said, and caught eyes with Ebony and Raya. Her voice rolled up and down, as though she had practiced a particular style of speaking. "But I'm sure you didn't. I mean, it's a long way to go to be put on a wait list." She made it sound like she was meaning to be nice, and even laughed as she looped her arm around Marla's waist, adding, "Scott and I got our daughter on the wait list when she was three months old."

Sonia's heart sank, but Marla grinned sideways at her as the women went on to chatter perkily about all the people they knew on the wait list.

They were heading back to the garden, Sonia in tow, when she remembered the cookies. "I brought ginger snaps," she said, holding the Tupperware out to Marla.

Claire peered over her shoulder. "Oh. Do those have sugar in them?"

Marla gave Sonia an apologetic grin. "Sorry, Sonia, we don't do sugar here."

"Or plastic," Claire said.

"Of course. I don't usually either... I'll just put them back in the car." Sonia felt a tightening sensation and turned quickly, catching her breath as she ducked her head and hurried away. Turning past a large oak with her head down, she slammed hard into someone who grabbed at her arm.

"Sorry," she said. "Excuse me." The man continued to hold her arm, looking at her for a beat too long, and she flushed. Great, she thought, she was now the kind of person that complete strangers felt instant concern for. When did all this private anxiety turn into out-there social anxiety?

"My fault entirely," he said. "That oak tree is a real blind corner. Let me walk you to the parking lot. That's where you're headed? I'm Scott, by the way. My daughter is River. I think I just met your husband and son. He's going to be a heartbreaker, that one."

She nodded, assuming he meant Jesse.

"You're sure you're okay?" He had let go, but was walking close to her, and when she didn't answer, he kept talking. "Here, have some water. So, welcome to Clifford. We moved out here from the West Coast, too. Cortez Island – you know, the uber-hippy one. We had goats out there, and here we're raising chickens and putting on puppet shows and churning butter."

She cocked an eye at him and he smiled. "Kidding. But just about the butter. The rest is all true. My partner is a freelance life coach and I'm an organic farming mentor. That's true, too. We may as well churn the butter."

Sonia grinned through her pre-panic tremors.

They reached her car and she leaned against it, letting her lungs fill and relax, fill and relax. She thought she'd be okay, but longed to sink down to the ground.

"Are those ginger cookies? I'm dying for sugar. My partner banned it from the house. Only local raw honey is allowed – which she eats by the jar. Let's have a seat, shall we?" He gestured to the silky grass below them.

They sat eating the snaps, talking. She looked up suddenly when she heard someone calling Scott's name. "I should go check on Bert and Jesse," she said, climbing to her feet. It felt like she had been sitting for a long time.

He stood up and they were just looking at each other, when Claire arrived.

"There you are!" She kissed Scott on the lips. "Oh, you met...sorry, I forget your name. I'm so bad with names!" She turned her face up to Scott's, laughing.

"Sonia," he said. "This is Sonia."

Claire's body turned to Scott and she said in a stagey whisper: "River is having a meltdown in the tree house and I need some backup."

Sonia and Scott looked toward the tree house, where they could see River hugging the base of the tree, swaying and appearing to sing to herself.

"Ah. Well. Looks like an emergency. It was really good to meet you, Sonia," Scott said and dipped his head to her. They walked away, Claire ducking under his arm and leaning her head on his shoulder. Sonia thought the angle of her neck looked painful.

After his week in hospital, after the cracked ribs, Bert missed several weeks of basketball. He went to the games anyway, sitting on the bench, while Sonia sat in the stands, watching him sit on the bench.

He started smoking pot in a stand of trees, off by himself. Sometimes he took acid or did mushrooms or E. He wouldn't touch alcohol, said he hated the smell. He didn't want to come to Sonia's house anymore, but wouldn't give a reason. He came to her swim meets, but when she looked up after a race she could never find him. Later, she would walk out of the school and find him in his truck in the parking lot, the air around him hazy. She would slip in beside him for the usual routine: a few words, a make-out session or covert sex, which would end up with him lying in her arms for a long time with music playing.

One time, though, as she opened the door, he asked: "Do you ever think about dying? I mean, like, wanting to die?"

She froze, one foot in the truck, the other on the ground. Somewhere, deep underneath his beauty – which she saw very sharply – was this part of him, this ticking bomb. She could tell a lot from his eyes and when she looked at them now, she felt scared. She was in over her head. She flashed in her mind to Mr. Sendak. Bert read this in her eyes and his one hand shot out and gripped her wrist. "Don't. Tell. Anyone," he said. "Just get in the car."

She didn't move and to her shock, Bert started crying – like, *weeping*. "Get in. Please," he managed to say.

She climbed up, her heart beating in her ears, and did what she knew how to do: hold him and kiss him and ask nothing.

"I have to get out," he said.

"Okay." She shifted her weight off him, but he shook his head.

"No. Out of his house."

"Oh. Is it—" her throat went dry. "Does he—" And that's when it happened: there was a second, just the briefest, tiniest opening, when she thought he might be willing her to ask. But what were the words? She stared at him, blinking, her mouth opening then closing, her brain wiped clear, until he reached out and laid one of his large, cool hands on her breast and said, "You're shaking."

"I am?"

"And you look white."

"I am white."

"Like sick. Are you going to be sick?"

She looked at him.

"It's okay. Come here." He pulled her into his warm body and held her until her breathing slowed. "Did you win your race?" he asked after a long stretch of quiet.

Her eyes flew open, she hadn't realized she had closed them, that she had almost fallen asleep. "Yeah. I did."

"Champion," he murmured, his chin in the muscular curve her strong shoulders formed. They fell asleep that way.

Bert was chatty as they drove home from the Forest School work party. He had talked with a lot of different parents and teachers and liked them well enough. That was the thing about Bert, he didn't let people too far in, but in superficial conversations he could be easy, jovial – probably it was the weed talking.

"Where'd you disappear to, anyway?" he asked.

"Oh, I was here and there."

He looked at her for a moment. "Hey, you know, I was thinking, maybe if you find work right away here, maybe I'd do this organic farming internship I was talking about with Claire. She and Scott invited us over—"

Sonia took in a quick breath. "We agreed you were going to work."

"Yeah, but, I just feel like, out here you don't need to work as much, you know? If you're growing your own food. Scott and Claire grow 65 per cent of their food and barter for most of the rest."

She set her jaw and then the panic that had subsided earlier in the day rose in her chest at full force, swelling hard against her rib cage. He just didn't understand, he never did, the work it took to be a grown-up. It all fell to her to hold their life together. She reached down for her cloth bag, but it wasn't there.

Bert was watching and one eye flickered to the back seat, checking on Jesse, who mercifully, had fallen asleep. "What do you want me to do?" he asked.

"I don't know, I don't know," was all she could say. She felt her throat narrowing and she looked at Bert, afraid.

"Is it going to pass?"

"I don't know!"

When she wheezed in a strangled breath, he pulled over and reached into his back pocket. "I'm calling Diana," he said. Sonia nodded and was about to tell him her phone number, but Bert had already tapped a button on his phone.

"Hey," he said. "It's me – I know I'm not supposed to call – just listen – Sone's having a bad attack and we don't have any of her stuff with us – Okay…okay." He held out the phone to Sonia. Sonia took it, still wheezing, but trying hard to sound steady, calm.

Diana coached her through the wave of anxiety, reminding her of her inner peace, her child-self. Her voice was soothing, and within a few minutes Sonia was responding to Diana's questions and Bert eased the car back onto the road. She stayed on the phone the whole way, Diana's kindness seeping through the phone, warming her. When they got home, Bert took his phone back and said he needed a walk.

"I thought you'd only gone to see her the once," Sonia heard herself say.

He stopped. "Yeah. Well, no. I mean, I guess I've seen her a little more than that." He turned and kept walking toward the lake. My God, he was a beautiful man, she thought. Just the way he was put together. He kept walking until the edges of him blurred and then were gone. She thought she should have fallen back into her panic attack then, some inner body within her braced for it. But the panic didn't come. The space around her felt suddenly abundant with oxygen.

A few days later, they took up Claire's invitation and went over to their farm. Their house was a modern structure of a clean and industrial cut, beside an aging, sagging barn.

"We plan to tear that down and reuse the materials in a more sustainable design," Claire said, touring them through the property in shiny rubber boots and denim overalls with mani-cured rips in the knees. "Then we can bring in some goats, or perhaps yaks."

Inside the house, Scott poured them all wine and they sat at a table that was a sleek slab of marble on rough-hewn legs. Sonia had bought a wicker basket of local cheeses and fruit at the farm-ers' market and Scott laid it out on a gleaming cutting board.

"This is so sweet of you," Claire said. "Isn't it just a luxury to eat something you haven't grown or made yourself?"

From across the table, Scott grinned at Sonia.

"Oh, totally," Bert was saying. "I mean, thank God someone knows how to make mozzarella 'cause I sure don't. Or mushrooms. Or maple syrup!"

Claire looked at him in surprise and laughed and Sonia knew what would happen then. Through sheer, dopey charm and good looks, Bert would have Claire acting like the girls back in high school. He was high as a kite, but as always, hiding it beautifully. He came off as relaxed, easily delighted. He'd never disclose anything about himself, but it wouldn't matter. Women like Claire wanted to talk about themselves, to him.

Jesse, who was playing shy with River, tugged on Sonia's pant leg and asked to go outside to the swings.

"Sure thing, Cowboy," she said, taking his hand and heading outside.

Scott followed a moment later, River on his back. "She thought she might show him a thing or two. She's a professional swinger."

Sonia nodded. The two kids were pumping their legs, their arcs criss-crossing as they gained altitude. The light around them was golden, as though an amber syrup had been poured over everything; it made their complexions seem rosy. It lit the barn and the fields. She watched Jesse's face, his thrill when the swing looped toward the earth and his lean form as he willed it back up, toes stretched to the pink sky.

"If you listen carefully," Scott said, "you can hear the lake from here."

Sonia tried to hear and suddenly became aware of the shape of her ears, felt as though she could feel them cupping the air, turning and tuning in. Slowly, beneath the metallic whine of the swing's joints, she could hear that hushing blur of sound. She had forgotten how here, in this part of the world, it was the background sound to life. Lately, her background noise had been an electrical hum – that is what constant anxiety sounded like. But the volume on her anxiety was turned down now: for some reason, it had been since she'd heard Bert say on the phone to Diana: "It's me."

Maybe once, she thought, she could have repaired them. If she had said to him that night in his car, Tell me about your dad. If she had insisted he tell her, then gone for help. But she hadn't. And then she hadn't again, each time the opportunity arose. When they graduated and she found him in an empty classroom with bloodshot eyes, unable to speak; when they moved into their first apartment and he arrived from his father's house with a truckload of boxes and a greenish bruise on his cheek. She'd seen that look in his eyes, pleading to not have to explain. Or had he been pleading for something else?

"There," Scott said, almost whispering. The light was becoming more like melted copper now. The trunks of the oaks beside the swings seemed to glow, almost lava-like, from within and Sonia tried to memorize this: the swish of the swings and Jesse's eyes alight and the sound in the near distance of the waves slipping onshore and receding. Such a softness came around her. She closed her eyes, too, and immediately, the sound of the water returned. Sonia felt her attention become granular; a rooting sensation occurred, as though she were being pinned into a new location, and she felt that her position in it was made possible by the sounds of the lake and by the feeling of Jesse, his free launch into the sky and his drop back down.

But also perhaps by the feeling of Scott standing beside her, so calmly. When she opened her eyes to glance over at him she realized he was just as present in this second as she was; it was like she could see him absorbing the sounds, the light, the joy of the children, her own energy perhaps.

"I wish every moment could feel like this," she said.

Scott opened his eyes and smiled at her, though his eyes seemed serious. "I hope – you'll feel at home here," he said, somewhat clumsily, as though he was trying to sort out his words.

"I do. Already."

"Please don't take it personally if Claire's a little sharp at the edges," he said in a bit of a rush. "I'm sure you'll get Jesse into the school if that's what you want."

Sonia shrugged. "We'll see."

"There are a lot of good, kind people there."

She looked at him and he met her eyes, then put his hands to his hips and squinted upward. "I mean, she's one of them. She's just – we're just going through a bit of a rough time."

"It's okay," she said. "I've developed some sharp corners myself."

"Oh, I don't think that can be true," Scott said, turning his face to hers. "You strike me as the complete opposite. You must be a water sign. A real fish."

She laughed, and he did, too, embarrassed at himself. "I don't usually talk like that," he said. "Or at least, not anymore."

"Not since you left Cortez?"

"Oh," he gazed out over the field, "since before that, to be honest."

Sonia nodded. She had to swallow at something hard forming in her throat.

She could so easily imagine Diana being a great comfort to Bert. Diana had a way of getting right to the heart of a person's problem. She could imagine them in her jasmine-scented office with the plush, vanilla ice cream-coloured couch and cozy lighting that somehow felt like candlelight. She would start out lightly enough, just tapping along, Bert being evasive, and then Diana hitting the nerve, finding the root of the problem and going for it, reassuringly, soothingly. And had he told her? Had he told her what he'd never told Sonia? Just because Diana had the courage to ask? She found she could imagine this as well. He might have been waiting for someone to make him tell his story all along. That horrible story, Sonia realized, she could not bear to hear. It came to her at once that she had not kept their pact of silence all these years solely for him.

She heard herself let out a long, slow breath. A wave of sadness rose up in her, then fell. "I used to be captain of my swim team," she said. "But I haven't been swimming in years. It started to feel a bit…overwhelming."

Scott was nodding. She looked at him, but he kept looking outward, the light turning his skin a pretty, neon pink. "It can be. It can be very overwhelming."

"I learned to swim in this lake, when I was Jesse's age."

He studied her a moment. "I think there is something particular about people who grow up on this lake," he said. "I've learned that since living here. One of the grandmothers at the school told me the French had a name for Lake Huron – *le mer douce*." He had a beautiful accent. "It means Freshwater Sea, or Gentle Sea. She told me that some consider it to have healing properties." He cleared his throat. "And that people in pain are drawn to it." His eyes flitted to her. "Sorry. I didn't mean to imply…"

Sonia had never heard this, but she pressed her fingertips to the corners of her eyes. "That feels about right." She could hear her voice beginning to give out.

"Sonia," he said, and turned to her. She tried turning her head, but he didn't look away.

She wasn't embarrassed. It was somehow easy to feel exactly as she needed to in front of him. "It's all right. I just don't want Jesse to see," she said, and absorbed as much of the water on her face as she could with her palms and the backs of her hands. "But it's all right. It's good that I do this."

Scott didn't say anything. She felt him delicately settle a warm hand on her back. It felt like a lifeline and she stood there crying in silence, feeling everything at the core of her slowly pool into the moment: she felt infused; a part of Jesse and the swing and the sounds, and the gold of the oak leaves and everything else the light touched as it flowed outward and outward until it reached the lake and the lip of the horizon and poured over. Continuing on.

GLORIOUS KINGDOM

Mom comes out into the backyard, the cordless phone in her hand – cell phones give you cancer – and she has a pitcher of cold licorice tea for us and says into the phone: "I'll think about it. I'll walk through the labyrinth and have a good think."

She is probably talking to Cedar, her best friend. Cedar used to be Mary-Anne, but changed it when they all picked new names. Mom is still Linda, except I heard her say on the phone "Luna" once and then when she turned around and saw me in the doorway, watched me for a moment and said, "I mean Linda."

Mom's on the phone a lot now because she's in a club called Earth Mother and they're making plans. Earth Mother used to be a club for moms who liked to garden and stuff, but now it's for radical environmental activists. I'm not exactly sure what that means, but I heard Mom say it to Cedar. Cedar said back the thing that's on all their T-shirts and the signs they made: *Protect the planet like you'd protect your kids! It's time for us to mother Earth!*

I am up in the kingdom. This is what we call our tree house. Gloria is climbing up the ladder.

"Princess Earth Mother wants to make a trade, King Luke," Gloria says, coming up with a kingdom name for my mom on the spot. "She's got sustenance."

I look at her.

"Cold tea and apple muffins."

I stroke my pretend beard. "How much does she want for them?"

"A couple nasturtium seeds."

"Deal."

Seeds are our money. That was my idea. What's more valuable than a seed? The Earth Mothers have a booth at the farmers' market where they sell seed packets and say speeches. "Hell No to Mon-san-to," Mom says to people walking past the booth. It's time for us to mother Earth! Nobody really stops to buy the seeds anymore, but in our kingdom, seeds are everything. Some are more valuable than others – a grass seed is like a penny; an orange seed a $20 bill.

My little sister Bea is queen. She made me. Gloria wanted to be the kingdom samurai. We said sure, but we're not allowed to play pretend with guns at our house and she said samurais use swords anyhow, so we checked it with Mom and she said no, we have to just use our words. So now Gloria is our samurai negotiator. She's pretty good, too. Mom says Gloria could talk her way out of a sealed nut.

Gloria climbs back down the ladder and makes the trade with Mom. Mom is watching me while this happens and she is also still on the phone. Our dog, Chalky, is beside her. Chalky used to stick to Dad like glue, but now it's Mom he sticks to. Mom pretends it annoys her and swats him away, but at night she pulls Chalky's slobbery head onto her lap when she sits on the couch.

I see her put the nasturtium seeds into her sweater pocket. She has this funny look on her face, like she's concentrating so hard on me. Once when I got to go on a two-day school camping trip, Bea looked at me that way. She said, "I'm trying rememberize your face in case you don't come back, Luke."

"Memorize, dummy," I said.

When Gloria wiggles back up through the trapdoor into the kingdom, muffins in her pockets, she says, "I know what Princess Earth Mother is thinking about. What she's talking about on the phone."

Gloria's a bit older – nine – and is always one step ahead of me. She's got some kind of bat phone connection to the adult world that I don't understand. When I'm at her house I notice her parents talking to her like she's a grown-up. "Where do you think the garbage goes when you're finished with it, Gloria? What would your solution be?" They ask that question a lot: "And what would your solution be, Gloria?"

"My parents told me," Gloria continues. "The Earth Mothers are protesting the construction at Heron Creek."

I've heard a little about it. Mostly from when Cedar and Mom were gardening together a couple of days ago and I was in my room in my window seat, reading my comics: Heron Creek is old growth and it would be a sin to cut it down for condos. It's a sacred place. That's what they said.

This doesn't seem like such a big thing. Protest is what Mom says Bea is doing when she won't drink kale juice.

"My dad said they're going to climb up in the trees and stay there until the bulldozers drive away."

"What?" I stop chewing. "How long will that take?"

"Ten years," Gloria says. "Or something like that."

"My mom wouldn't leave us that long," I say. But as soon as I say it I'm not so sure anymore. Mom gets tired now and sometimes at bedtime, when she reads me *Danny Champion of the World*, she says, Can we stop here for the night? way before she should, and folds the corner of the page over and goes to the bathroom for a while.

"And they're bringing bike locks and stuff," Gloria says, "to like, lock their arms to the wheels of the bulldozers." She squints up at the sky, as though trying to remember more. "And they're going to sneak in barricades so the bulldozers and the police can't get in."

"Police?" I get this funny feeling in my stomach and Gloria says, "Don't be a cry baby. The Earth Mothers are all sacrificing themselves for the forest. It's a noble quest."

"I'm not crying. I'm just concerned. About Bea. Who will look after her if something bad happens to Mom?"

Gloria shrugs. "You, I guess. Or maybe you'll get adopted."

Now my stomach tightens hard, like somebody's fist got inside it and is bunching up all my organs. I don't want Mom to go! I don't want to get adopted. I look out the treehouse window, but Mom isn't there in the spot where she was. I don't want Gloria to think I'm a baby so I say, "I'm going to get more muffins."

But Gloria steps in front of the trapdoor. "Don't be selfish. What do you think is more important? You or the whole forest?"

Behind Gloria, through the window in the kingdom, I spot my mom walking slowly through the blackberry labyrinth. She is far away and her back is to me, but I imagine the brave look she might have, deciding to leave us for the forest. Like in movies when the hero has to do something they know they should but don't want to. Or when Dad was still sick and Mom would come home from the hospital alone and say he seemed all right.

When my mom comes around a curve in the labyrinth, I see her face. She looks like a real princess. Maybe even like a real elf princess. I feel sick to my stomach. If Mom didn't get so mad about pushing, I would push Gloria now! I feel so weird – sad and mad at the same time.

Then, suddenly, an idea slides into my brain like magic.

"I'll go with her."

Gloria looks at me, her eyes going big. "Oh, don't even go there," she says in a voice like a teenager girl on TV – on the kind of show Mom won't let us watch. Then she pauses and her eyes go fuzzy. "She won't let you. It's too dangerous. She might not even want you there." But it sounds almost like a question and she's not even looking at me. "But you could sneak there before them," she says slowly, still staring at something behind me, "and be waiting when they climb up… It would only be scary 'til they got there."

"She will so let me," I say. "And I'm not scared. I'll take Chalky with me." But I am scared. I try to imagine running away, climbing up the great big trees at Heron Creek by myself. How would I even get to Heron Creek? We used to go before, for family hikes, but Dad would drive us and Mom would turn up the radio and turn around and silly dance in her seat to make me laugh.

And even if I got to Heron Creek, how would I get Chalky and Bea up the tree? And how would we live there? And what if Gloria is right and Mom doesn't really want me there? What if she means it's time for *her* to mother Earth – like, instead of us. But Mom wouldn't leave me! She loves me. She says so all the time. Stupid Gloria, I hate her!

After a moment Gloria's eyes focus back in on mine. "Yeah. Okay," she says. Then she fingers a muffin out of her pocket and shoves it into her mouth, the whole thing, and then she can't close her mouth around it and some squishes out and she laughs, which makes more plop out. "Was that a good decision, Gloria?" she asks in a pretend grown-up voice that is all muffled because of the muffin.

Mom stands under the kingdom and looks up at us through the trapdoor.

"You hungry, Kiddo?" she asks me.

I feel hot in my eyes and jerk my head away. "No."

"Well, it's getting late. I think Gloria needs to go home and you should come down for some supper." She has a basket of green beans that she picked in the garden under one arm. She holds the basket up to me, like maybe this will make me want to come in for dinner or like she wants me to take it.

I get this feeling that I get lately, even before I knew Mom was going to the forest to stop the bulldozers. Like I want to shout "Come back" but it's stupid 'cause she's right here. I could reach down and touch her, almost.

Mom lowers her arms and looks back toward the labyrinth then she turns and walks toward the house.

"You're being very brave," Gloria says to me. "Princess Earth Mother will appreciate you supporting her mission."

"Yeah." I rub my nose on the shoulder of my T-shirt.

Gloria comes to stand directly in front of me and whispers: "Don't tell her you know about the mission. It's supposed to be top secret."

"But then how come your parents told you?"

"Huh?"

"You said your parents told you."

"Well, they did. Accidentally. I overheard them talking about it, is what I meant to say. We're not supposed to know. So don't say anything to your mom. The princess, I mean. Okay?" She thrusts out a hand and when I don't take it immediately, sticks out her hip and sighs. "Think of the bigger picture here, Luke."

In the kitchen, after Gloria goes home, I drag the stool over to the sink and step up to wash my hands. Mom is beside me, reaching her arm into a cupboard for the cloth napkins. She tosses them onto the table and winks at me. She's slid back into regular Mom, the before-Dad-got-sick Mom. She slides in and out.

"You're looking pretty serious," she says, and when I don't answer she shrugs and looks to the couch and asks, "Do you know where Chalky is?"

Bea stumbles in from the living room. Her hair looks like a bird's nest sticking out from the side of her head. "Glorious kingdom," she mumbles, barely awake.

Mom tilts her head and grins. Bea is always saying silly things out of nowhere and it makes Mom and me laugh. She scoops Bea up and Bea lays her head on Mom's shoulder, her eyes slowly closing.

"Mumma," she murmurs, and twists a hunk of Mom's shiny hair around her fist. She rubs her face into Mom's neck and sighs. Mom closes her eyes and makes the same kind of sound, but slower and greyer.

I see my mom, waving to us, then climbing up a tree, her green, cloth backpack swinging from her shoulders, Cedar and the other Earth Mothers are already up in the giant old trees, reaching their hands out to her. In my mind, she is smiling, like everything is easy again. Like it's no big deal. Like it's better to go live there.

I jump off my stool and run over to her. "Mom!" I throw both arms around her legs and press my hot face into her tummy. I want to tell her not to slide away, but my throat feels like I swallowed a whole hard gumball.

"What's this?" Mom asks, sounding surprised. "Luke?" She lowers slowly to one knee, still holding Bea. "What's the matter, Kiddo?"

She is looking straight at me and I swallow the gumball a little. "Don't go up in the trees and leave us here." I'm crying now, tears on my face as warm as bathwater. My nose gets really snotty and I rub it against Mom's leg, leaving a shiny trail.

Mom runs her hand through my hair. "Up in the...?" She frowns, her eyebrows bunched together, and then suddenly her face changes, opens and falls. "That Gloria," she says, and wraps her free arm around me, hugs me tight, rubs my back. "Luke. You know Gloria likes to play tricks on you. Stop crying, Baby. Tell me." Her voice is soft and her breath is warm in my face and smells like sweet tea.

I stop crying, but it feels nice and warm squished into Mom so I stay. I reach my arm around and pat her back, then rest it on Bea's leg. "She said she knew what you said on the phone."

Mom looks at me, puzzled.

"What you said to Cedar, about 'I'll think about it,'" I say.

"Oh." Mom shakes her head. "I was talking to Gloria's mom, actually. She was—" Mom stops. "What did Gloria say to you, Luke?"

Bea lifts her head suddenly and says: "I told you. What Gloria said was she's going to Heron Creek, to be queen of her own kingdom."

Mom puts a hand up to her mouth, then looks at me and brings it back down. "Would she do that?"

I think of Gloria's face when I was telling her I would run away and climb the tree and take Chalky. "Um. She might."

Mom's face goes greyish-yellowish, like when right after Dad was gone and Mom got shaky and puked all over the floor on her way to the bathroom.

Bea tips her sleepy head back, hair fluffing out around her face. "She gave me seven tomato seeds for Chalky," she says, then squinches her eyes as though she suspects she's been tricked: "Is that how much he costs for real?"

Mom gets quick and bright. I can see her making a list in her head of what to do. First, she calls Gloria's house and doesn't get an answer. "Shit," she says, hanging up the phone. Then she winks at me. "Sorry. Emergency swear. Okay, well, I guess we should drive over there. See if anybody's home."

Bea sticks out her pouty lip. "Chalky's going to be so mad at me," she says.

The phone rings and Mom lunges for it. "Deb?" she asks as she picks it up. Deb is Gloria's mom.

But it's not Deb. It's Cedar, I hear Mom say, and she must be telling Mom something that makes her worry, because she puts her hand up over one cheek and says, "Oh God. Emergency swear." It's quiet for a second as she listens, then she says, "She called me today and said she and Jerry were serious about it and if something happened to them, would I watch Gloria for a while. But I didn't say yes. Christ. They've gone full eco-terrorist, that's what. And now they're at the site and Gloria's run away to find them and she took our damn dog." She rubs at her forehead with her eyes scrunched closed and when she opens them and sees me looking at her, turns to face the other way and talks in a quieter voice. "Cedar, I've told you, I'm not prepared to – It's just different now. I'm all they've got… It's *not* selling out." Quiet again, and she makes a face like she smells something bad. "What do you mean more publicity?" She's looking at me and then at Bea and I think Cedar's not talking the whole time, it's just that Mom is thinking the whole time. "We're talking about a child," she says very softly into the phone then hangs up.

She looks at me. "Luke, honey, how do you think Gloria would get herself and Chalky to Heron Creek?"

We have to get in the car fast. Mom tosses us a jar of trail mix and tells us to snack, and when we get to Gloria's house she tells us to stay in the car. She comes out a minute later looking pissed. "Nobody home."

When she gets back in the driver's seat, she puts both hands on the wheel and squeezes until it looks like her knuckles are going to pop out of the skin. "Okay," she says after a minute. "Okay. We're going to drive to Heron Creek the way Gloria might walk. Everybody look for Gloria and Chalky. I called the police so they're looking too, but let's find her first."

"Is this a game?" Bea asks and Mom says, "Yes! A game!" and Bea says, "Dumb game."

Mom turns on the radio and starts pressing buttons. She stops when it comes to a man talking about the prime minister, and then he stops talking about that and starts talking about a forest fire up North, and then he stops talking about that and starts talking about environmentalists at Heron Creek.

"Shush!" Mom says, even though no one is talking, and turns up the volume.

The man says something about some people being radical, and then I don't understand anything else he says except that my skin prickles like when you know someone is about to do something stupid or dangerous, like kids on the playground equipment jumping from way too high up.

Mom says "Shit" and then squints out at the road. "You see them?"

"Nope," I say and pretend like I've been looking hard, too. But really, I've been looking at Mom, who fiddles with the radio a bit more, looking for another station now that the man has stopped talking. She's looking out the window, but I feel like she's thinking about something besides Gloria and Chalky. Sometimes she'll look at the place in the kitchen where Dad used to stand or at his chair at the table – well, not at the chair, but at the place where his face would be if he was sitting in the chair. Then she gets small in her body and away go her eyes.

"What are they going to do once they get to Heron Creek?" I ask.

She doesn't answer. She's biting her lip and leaning forward in her seat, her shoulders scrunched up high. I ask her again.

She takes a deep breath. "It was supposed to be a tree sit, but some of the Earth Mothers think that's not enough anymore."

"Gloria said they're bringing locks and stuff."

We come to a red light and Mom slides forward in her seat, scans left to right. "Gloria's parents should be more concerned about Gloria."

"But will it work?"

She sighs, and then shrugs. "Maybe. Hopefully. If it's done right."

"Will Deb and Jerry do it right?" I ask.

Mom sniffs. "I don't know. You need a cool head, a team. They've gone a bit rogue."

I know what rogue means. "Rebels," I say.

Mom looks at me, surprised. "Wackos," she says, after a moment.

"But," I search my brain for something I've heard Mom say before, when people make excuses for why they can't stop and listen to her speeches or read her pamphlets, "if we don't protect the planet, who will?"

Mom looks at me for so long that the light changes and the car behind us honks.

We get to Heron Creek, no sign of Gloria or Chalky on the way. Mom doesn't park right – just swerves in and stops the car, jumps out. "We can get in and get out before anything starts," she says, kind of talking to herself. "Look for Gloria or her parents." Her hands are fast on Bea's buckles in the car seat and she tells me to be quick. We don't even slide the van door shut, we just start running.

Our shoes on the boardwalk sound like the wooden xylophone at school. The boardwalk curves into the forest like it's a long wooden tongue hanging out of the mouth of a beast made of leaves. Heron Creek looks like when I lie on my belly in the yard and peek through the blades of grass, down into the dirt and see green and yellow and white all blurred together and my nose fills with the smell of dirt and rocks and bugs and grass. In Heron Creek, the trees are fat and so high you have to tilt your head all the way back to see up to the top. Vines grow on the tree trunks and moss grows on the vines. It is green in your eyes and nose and I can even feel green on my skin, damp and soft.

Suddenly there is the sound of shouting. "Get out of the park!" someone is yelling at us.

Mom stops running and grabs my hand and Bea's. Bea falls over, but gets up yelling: "Chalky!"

Then it's fast. Two people dressed in black run so fast past us that Bea gets knocked over again, and one of them turns to look back at her and I see a walkie-talkie on his belt. Or I hear it. It crackles and snaps. There's a badge and that's when I feel scared because I know if the police are here then someone did something bad. Or maybe it's bad that we're here and they'll make Mom go to jail. And then the crackling and snapping gets really loud, like pop, pop, pop! and Mom pulls me and Bea off the boardwalk into the ferns and holds us down.

"Shit, shit, shit," I hear, but I can't see anything 'cause Mom is pressing me down so hard it hurts my neck. The ground is wet and I can feel it making the knees of my pants all wet too. Something slides underneath my shins, like a smushed mushroom or slimy moss. When I wiggle, she pushes harder, but then

I twist my head and see more black shoes running on the board-walk and I hear a loud explosion and yelling and it starts to get really scary, so I squeeze my eyes shut but then my eyelids flash and I open my eyes again: there is a funny green colour all around, like a lightning bolt bright green on the shiny green leaves and white zingy green in the little bit of sky where the trees don't touch.

"Get out of there!" someone yells. Another police officer, a lady with a yellow ponytail. "You get out of there!" She runs to us and grabs Mom's arm. "It's not safe." She glares at Mom. "Are you a protestor?"

"No!" Mom says, "Well – no. I mean—" She looks panicky and tightens her arms around me and Bea.

The police officer looks at me. "Why are these children here?" She gives my mom a mean, angry look. "You crazy activists! Take these children home and keep them safe."

I expect Mom to shout back, to zing her with one of the good slogans, but instead I hear Mom make this terrible sound and when I look at her, her face is all red and her eyes look very sad. "I know that!" she says. "I know."

The police officer holds out her arm and Mom grabs at it to pull us all up. "Do you know them?" she asks. "Do you know what else they might have with them? Any weapons?" Her walkie-talkie crackles and she pulls it to her mouth. "Whatcha got?" she says into it. She spreads her arms wide and pushes us back toward the parking lot. Bea keeps calling for Chalky and the police lady turns her head away from her walkie-talkie for a moment. The voice sounds like when our radio isn't quite on the right station. "Who's Chalky?" she barks at my mother.

"There's a girl. A nine-year-old named Gloria," Mom says. "She's about this tall, with long brown hair, brown eyes. I thought we could find her, but…that's your job." She scoops Bea up and squeezes my hand and turns around and we start walking away. All of a sudden, there is so much popping and sparks fly into the sky, zinging bright green. It's so loud, I put my hands over my ears and tuck my head into Mom. It seems like it goes on forever. Everybody's face is green and the sky, too, and I can see Bea is yelling but it's so loud I can't even hear her.

It's so loud and crazy we all jam into each other, like a statue of our family, all still, made of stone. Then all of a sudden Mom squeezes my hand in a way that I know she wants me to bring my head out from under her arm and look at her face. It's all pale and glowing at the same time, and I see her mouth move: "Fire. Works," she says slowly, so I can read her lips, and I can tell by her face she's confused, but wants me to believe I can be relieved. Finally, the popping stops and everything goes quiet except Bea who is still screaming – screaming so loud her voice breaks. I think she must be calling for Chalky, but then in the sudden quiet, we hear her:

"…Gloooooor-ia's Kingdom!"

Mom takes my hand and Bea's and ducks her head and starts walking with us quickly. The police lady is shouting at us but Mom just walks faster, and when we get back to the van she pushes us in the back seat and climbs in with us and pulls us onto her lap and hugs us for a long time. One of us is shaking a bit and I know it won't be Bea, but it could be me or Mom or both of us.

"I'm sorry that was so scary," she says when she lets go. She has a bit of black stuff under her eye, like when she cries when we're watching a movie and it gets to the sad part or like when we're at the grocery store and somebody says to her, "It's just not fair. He was such a good person – and so young."

"I'm sorry. That was stupid of me. I shouldn't have taken you in there." She looks at me. "I'll never do that again."

Bea wants more trail mix. Or chicken fingers. She scrambles into her car seat herself and clicks the buckle. "Where do we go now?" she asks.

Mom wipes the back of her hand along the black smudge. "Your dad used to keep me in line on stuff like this. He used to balance me out. He had this calm about the future – no need to get upset. I don't know how he did it. He just had this unending faith that things would work out and he always knew where to draw the line between doing enough and going too far and now that he's gone, I just find it hard—"

I grab Mom's face with both hands and turn it to me. I think of that thing Gloria says when she wants me to stop talking about something, the words from the high school show. "Don't even go in there."

She frowns and shakes her head as much as she can with me holding it tight. "I'm not. We won't go back in. I promise."

Bea kicks the back of the seat in front of her. "Don't *go* there, dummy," she corrects me, and Mom looks at her for a minute, then at me, and nods slowly.

"Right. You're right." She sits up straight.

There's a sudden knock on the van window and we all jump. It's Deb, Gloria's mom.

"Deborah!" my mother yells, in the voice she uses for me when I'm in trouble.

Deb tells my mom that Gloria came home with Chalky, so they all turned around to walk him back to our house, but he got loose on the way and now they don't know where he is. They've been out driving around, looking for him and trying to get hold of us, and thought maybe we'd be here.

"But you don't use a cell phone," she finishes.

"You've got Gloria?" Mom asks and Deb nods.

"Gloria is with you?"

"Yes," Deb says again.

"Take her home, Deborah."

Then Mom doesn't say goodbye or anything, rolls up the window and gets into the front seat and we drive away. When I look behind us, Deb is watching our car, looking unsure about where she should go next.

On the way home, we roll our windows back down and call out Chalky's name. It starts to get a little bit dark out. Bea's asleep, her mouth hanging open. We pull into our driveway and Mom turns off the car, but neither of us move.

"Mom?" I say.

She looks at me and reads my mind. "Chalky's not afraid of the dark, Kiddo."

Her voice sounds good. Normal. I feel like maybe she's right.

I remember one time when we were blowing bubbles in the backyard in our little blow-up pool and Mom said, "Watch this, guys" and when Dad blew the bubbles, she dipped her finger into the pool water and then held it out, and this one big bubble came floating down and landed on her shiny finger like a baby bird landing on a branch in the rain. It was beautiful, that rainbow ball, glassy on my mom's finger, her hand with the light purple veins showing through. Behind the bubble, her face was calm and like cream. It was like a magic trick – not just the bubble catch, but the look on her face. The sureness that felt like it was being beamed down to her and out to us.

She has that look on her face now. She wraps one of my hands inside her two cool, still hands. "We're going to sit tight, the three of us, and wait for Chalky. We're just going to wait it out." She nods at me, her eyes looking into mine. "He'll find us."

NORTHERN TETHER

The first time Derek asked her a question, Marion lied to him. Because his question felt like a trap. And because he wore an earring.

They were at the choir's spring concert party. Styrofoam cups of neon pink lemonade. Someone handed her a cup filled to the lip, wrapped in a floral paper napkin. She watched others chatting giddily in clusters and couplets, high from their church basement performance in front of spouses and children. She kept lifting the cup to her mouth, absently, then remembering the foul colour, lowering it, careful not to spill.

Derek appeared. Marion had already noticed him at practice, though she had only joined a month ago, in May. At that time, a fine lace of dirty snow still covered the streets, and Marion knew she'd gone too long without being social outside of work. Derek: a tenor, if not tone deaf, then completely indifferent to melody. Curly hair, fumbling down his neck, flipped up. He sported the look that, after six months in the Yukon, Marion recognized as a local male motif: Carhartts, flannel button-up, pickup truck. A fuck-the-man-but-help-your-neighbour demeanour. Ridiculous smile: it took up a third of the available space on his face.

"Love or money?" Derek asked, sidling up to her, near a card table piled with Nanaimo bars and paper plates of cold cuts. All inedible, Marion decided. Yellow food dye in the bars, sweaty rolls of baloney.

He leaned in closer, smiling, smelling of cloying sweet-clean drugstore soap. Something called "Natural Pine Fresh." Natural Pine Fresh *was* the air up here. She had a brief, weird moment where she imagined men walking out their doors with their armpits exposed, or scooping the air up in their hands to splash on their cheeks after shaving. He was waiting for her.

"I mean, did you move up here for love or money? 'Cause I can sure as hell tell you're not under the spell of the Yukon."

Marion blinked. "Love," she said, believing this might at least prevent him from flirting with her.

"Really?" He drew the word out slowly, sing-songy, but then grinned to soften the tease. "Well, who's the lucky fellow? Another singing compadre?" He bounced on the balls of his feet.

"What makes you think I don't like it up here?"

"Oh, what your face is doing most of the time." He tightened his lips and made his eyes small – in a way that Marion had to admit looked the way her face often felt. "And you hate all the songs we sing in choir."

This was true. The choir director was freshly transplanted from down south. People who were new here, Marion had observed, would either assimilate enthusiastically or spend the winter alone in their quiet houses and be driven to do something just to do something come spring, such as joining the community choir.

The choir director was the Ultimate Assimilation Enthusiast. She had picked only songs with "Northern" in the title, or with poetic references to ravens and the aurora borealis. She had wholeheartedly joined the Can-Can Line – a ludicrous nod to the Yukon gold rush history of whorehouses and strippers.

Marion found this grossly anti-feminist and settler-centric. The choir director had been an instant hit.

Marion, on the other hand, couldn't muster the enthusiasm – she'd chosen to chance living in the Yukon for a year because she knew she needed a change. And she had once seen a post-card: teal blue mountains, bubblegum-pink fireweed popping against the teal. A black thread of river with a carved-out canoe banked at a bend. The canoe was empty, and Marion had imagined herself floating along the river into a world more ancient than the city she lived in then. She imagined the thin trees in the photograph had roots that reached like blue veins all the way to the heart of the earth.

"I was hoping we might sing about something other than the North," Marion said to Derek.

He popped a marbled cheese cube into his mouth and grinned, eyes fastened on her. Then he spat the cube discreetly into his napkin, and said: "Oh, that's bad."

Marion blinked at him rapidly.

He sipped water and swished it through his cheeks. "But this *is* the North."

What does that mean, exactly? Marion wanted to ask, but didn't. He wouldn't understand. Blythe would get it, though: the Northern self-references were too self-aggrandizing, parochial. Marion had seen it in every Whitehorse art gallery, every pamphlet advertising a cultural event. Even in the business names: Raven Records, Northern Lights Lingerie, the Sled Dog Pub. With each repetition she'd felt the Yukon become more and more of a packaged story; what once had loomed expansive in her mind had since been reduced to the size and profundity of a tourist trinket. The Yukon, the idea of it, could be dangled from a key chain if one had a few cents to spare.

Unable to quell her irritation, she said: "Well, that must mean there's something seriously wrong with me. If I'm not under the spell, I mean."

Derek snorted. "There's something seriously wrong with us all. That's why some of us came here; we were banished – by someone in our past, by ourselves, by society at large. And now we are free to be seriously wrong. No one checks on the Yukon; it's too far away. After a while that kind of freedom gets addictive and you'll never leave."

Marion raised her cup and lowered it. In her short time here, she had learned this was a cornerstone in the myth of the Yukon, and it too, reduced rather than enlarged her experience the more it was rehashed. "Yes, I've heard that before."

He widened his eyes and she looked away, saying, "I'm just here for a year-long contract with the government." And when his look didn't change, she added: "I'm not staying." He kept smiling, watching her. She found herself looking at his lips, frowning, shaking her head slightly.

"So," he said suddenly, "who's not checking on you?"

Her hand went to her mouth, tipped back the lemonade. She spluttered messily. She had to excuse herself to go to the bathroom. She had not expected him to go for the jugular like that.

After the choir concert, Marion walked home alone. Her rental house was a squat wooden purple box with a few shingles still nailed to the tar-papered roof, a cracked front window like an injured eye, and a lilac door that she had to kick open with considerable force in cold weather. The house was sinking slowly into the permafrost, tilting the floors. It looked like something between a playhouse and a haunted house – a hybrid dreamed up by an unhinged child.

Now that it was June, scrub grass bristled against the foundation of the house. As she let herself through the gate, dull purple caught her eye and she squatted beside a flower. It was a single crocus, but not like the ones she knew from back home in Victoria. There, crocuses were light, bright, and delicate, the first tiny petals of spring materializing in the mists of February. Easy to pluck. But this crocus was a fat, toad-like creature, stubbing through the earth, still rank with frost easing out. She imagined the flower gasping for breath as it reached air, and belching. As though the journey through the hardness of the ice and earth here could only be earned by the toughest of flowers. She didn't pick it; she imagined that if she tried she would tug and tug, but never be able to un-anchor the thick roots like muscles, their hoary grip firm on the earth.

Inside, she reached for the phone in the kitchen. It was the old kind of telephone, attached to the wall with a twisted cord that hung down, tethering her to one place. As though in acceptance of this, the landlady had positioned an armchair reupholstered in crushed velvet beside the phone. Marion liked to sit in the chair when she made her phone calls, always to the same number.

She pinched the phone to her chin with her shoulder. One hand poured hot water into a teapot, the other fished around in a drawer for the jar of leaves and the little perforated ball – Blythe had always call it a "tea egg" – to put the leaves in. A sudden vicious crack made Marion drop the phone and the egg. She squinted into the back of the drawer and saw a mousetrap squeezed shut over a tea bag in its dusty envelope. Must have been left by the previous tenant. She stretched her fingers, curled them into her palms, snatched the phone off the floor.

"Sorry about that, Blythe," she said. "I almost mouse-trapped my right hand! Anyway…please call me." She waited a moment, listening, then hung up.

Marion searched around on the floor for the tea egg. She finally saw it rolling out of the kitchen and down the hallway like a runaway, obeying the slant of the house.

Marion walked down the street for coffee the morning after the choir concert. Not far from her crooked purple house was another crooked purple house, but this one was a grocery store. Or some kind of store. It sold locally made dresses sewn from faded quilts, soya sauce, toothpaste, and – impossibly – very good dark chocolate. When Marion discovered this, she knew she'd make it through the winter. It was also the one place to get a passport photo taken and had a tiny espresso machine behind the till that offered the only macchiato in town.

Marion went to the store once a week, around eight in the morning, to get her espresso. Afterwards she would pick out one of the expensive bars of chocolate. Back in Victoria, she and Blythe, both avid home cooks, had considered themselves choco-late connoisseurs. There was a shop in Victoria that imported some of the best chocolate from around the world. They'd buy a few at a time then sit at their kitchen table with a notebook and snap off small squares. "Jammy," Blythe would say. Or vegetal, smoky, hint of wildflower. In her thin, sloped handwriting, she wrote down Marion's impressions as well. Marion thought she had the better palate, but she loved how Blythe would hold her pen poised over the lines of the notebook, watching Marion carefully work the chocolate around her mouth. Blythe's attention, the quietness as it melted down to the sweet, soft, bitter heart of it. And the way she made sure she wrote Marion's words just as she had said them. There was a seriousness to the ritual that gave Marion a deep pleasure. When Blythe moved out, Marion thought Blythe might ask to take the notebook with her, but she did not.

A big woman named Shelly owned the store. She had frizzy hair razored into a mullet that gleamed gunmetal grey under the fluorescent lights. She wore faded pink Crocs, revealing deeply grooved skin on her heels that reminded Marion of the shingles on her roof. When Shelly saw Marion approaching, she made a show of getting up heavily from her stool, walking on stiff legs to the back corner, and firing up the espresso machine. Marion marvelled at her oldness: it seemed as though her bones were made of wood, her skin of paper. But the eyes glittered – they were hot black stones from the centre of the earth.

"You know how much this machine costs if it breaks down?" Shelly asked Marion.

"No, I don't."

Shelly looked hard at her. "I have to send down to Vancouver for parts."

She kept her eyes on Marion as she ground the espresso beans and tamped them into the portafilter, a massive elbow winging up briefly and setting the wrinkled flesh under her arms wobbling.

Marion found her eyes hard to look into, but was also hesitant to look away from. Was she an Elder? Marion wondered. She couldn't quite pin an age on her, but guessed 83 to 90. She imagined asking out loud the questions in her mind: Shelly – can I ask you – what makes an elder an Elder? A particular age or a kind of possession of wisdom? What kind of wisdom? But no, she couldn't ask this woman whose heart, Marion intuited, was both larger and tougher than hers. She looked like a person who had burrowed downward, then upward, through many layers of sadness. Marion did not want to guess what that might have been, but she felt an aura around her, a protective aura, like the rings of Saturn.

She did not assume that the sadness was cultural, although it could have been, and Marion felt a cautiousness around even thinking that. What little could she understand? Or had the knowledge to be compassionate about, and how? Since moving to the Yukon, she had been taking history books out of the sparse local library, but for some reason this did not seem like quite the right place to learn what she suddenly understood she was so ignorant of. Sitting quietly and listening for weeks or months or years might be the right way to learn, she thought. She wanted Blythe there to air her questions to. Blythe who never judged, and never really answered either, but at least made Marion feel as though her deepest curiosities were more than vapour.

The espresso poured out in a thin cord and still Shelly watched Marion. "This is not a café," Shelly said, chunking the espresso cup down on the counter for Marion. It was a beautiful dark shot with a layer of velvety crema on top. It made Marion think of a palomino's coat, gleaming in the sun. She noticed Shelly said café the way the French do – a short, clipped *cuh* followed by a more drawn out, soft *fay*.

Marion wanted to say, yes, but you are the only person in town who makes a decent espresso, but worried it would sound too familiar, too ingratiating. Instead, she nodded at Shelly too enthusiastically. "Yes, I know. I'll just sip this quickly. Outside," she added and stepped out to the curb, still nodding.

She stopped short when she saw him, a drop of espresso sloshing over the side of the cup to paint her thumbnail. Derek was on the sidewalk, hands in pockets, toothpick in mouth. "Oh! Hey there, Hater," he said cheerfully.

"Excuse me?"

"Haters gonna hate," Derek said, by way of explanation. "You know Taylor Swift?" Marion looked at him blankly. Of course she knew Taylor Swift; anyone who'd passed by a radio in the past 10 years would. But Derek took her blankness as ignorance and began humming a nasally, tuneless version of what could have been any of the pop star's songs. Marion studied the sidewalk.

"Anyway, she wears that shirt in one of her videos. I love it: Haters gonna hate. Girl power. Am I right?"

Marion frowned, and tried fetching around in the ether for his line of thought. "Because... I hate it here?"

"Uh-huh." Derek nodded vigorously. "I like your hairdo."

Her hand flew up to her head. She had a neat, geometrical bob, a bit hipsteresque, meant to convey some kind of self-aware preppiness. When she'd gone to a local hairdresser for a trim, the woman had called her style "urban." Marion said to Derek: "It's not a hairdo; it's just hair."

Derek tongued the toothpick from one cheek to the other. "So, what do you do anyway?" he asked. "For work."

"Communications," she said.

"Ironic."

"Pardon?"

"You fish?"

Marion looked behind her and saw Shelly watching, arms folded over her ledge of bosom. Marion looked back to Derek quickly. "Um. No."

"Well!" Derek flashed his teeth, the toothpick protruding. "I'll take you to Fish Lake. Just out of town. Got a rod?"

"No."

"Perfect. How about tomorrow morning? Which house is yours anyway?"

Marion blinked, trying to work out how she was suddenly making arrangements to be picked up by Derek. To go fishing. From behind, Shelly said: "The purple one." When she turned she saw Shelly pointing down the street, through the clump of thin pines that hid Marion's house.

"Perfect," Derek said again. "I'll pick you up after breakfast." He started to walk away, then threw an arm up and without turning around, called out, "Cheers, Shelly."

"Cheers," Shelly replied in a flat monotone.

Marion set her cup on the counter and then quick-stepped to the sidewalk, feeling a bit buzzy, probably from the espresso.

Back at home, she paused to stare at a clipping of Halle Berry on the refrigerator door. Berry had been 45 at the time, and her photo signified a pact Marion and Blythe had made.

"If we're both still single when we're 45, we'll call a spade a spade," Blythe had sighed the day she stuck the clipping to the fridge with a magnet. "We'll live together for the rest of our lives. We'll drink old-fashioneds and eat pho and make fried chicken. We won't think about adoption or go out on dates. Look at Halle: gorgeous, courageous, single."

Marion was pretty sure Halle had a boyfriend, and a child, but still, Blythe's declaration brought her heady relief. Forty-five was a visible destination, a not-too-far horizon, which, when reached, meant she could at last stop meeting with men she found unpalatable, feigning interest, updating her parents on her pathetic love life. She would tell them and herself that so and so had seemed intelligent, had a nose for wine. No. They didn't really. They were always unappealing men who provided her with nowhere near the same amount of easy contentment as a day spent with Blythe. There was always something unacceptable – a fondness for fast food, a large mole on the neck with a black hair, clipped, but still, there.

On Marion's fridge in the purple house, Halle Berry was beside a photograph of Blythe's baby girl. It was outdated, but Marion still liked to look at it, touch her finger to the small ears and stare, not realizing she was smiling at the tiny pink nose. After some moments, she took in a jagged breath and remembered she'd come to the fridge for yoghurt.

Sometimes she scrolled through the most recent emails she had received from Blythe. They were from almost a year ago. *It's like crossing an ocean to a new continent. Like moving to Europe*, Blythe had written, trying to explain motherhood to Marion. *Life is pretty much the same, yet completely different and unfamiliar.*

The baby, Lila, had been unplanned. A pregnancy despite birth control in the first few months of Blythe's relationship with an older man named Tomas. Blythe had met him on an online dating site. Too early in the relationship, she began telling the story of how he had not wanted a second date, but then they ran into each other at the grocery store several days after it was clear he was never going to call her back, and ended up talking for an hour by the tomatoes.

"Can you imagine?" Blythe said, hands smoothing over her rounded belly. "And now a year later, here we are!" This was in the third trimester, after Tomas had come back.

He was a construction worker. Small, wooden objects around his cabin – boxes with tiny hinges, a curved, golden-hued high chair for the baby – showed that his true passion was for woodworking and that the square lines of the condos he built in Victoria were suffered through. He spoke very little, but when he did, it was usually against something, Marion noticed, as though he found his footing in the world by seeking traction.

At first, he was against the pregnancy yet also, unfairly, against abortion. It didn't matter; the transformation began for Blythe in the moment she and Marion stood in their apartment bathroom together watching the plus sign appear on the stick.

"Oh my God, Mare: I'm a mother," Blythe had whispered. She laid the kit down carefully on the lip of the sink, as though jostling it might reverse the verdict.

The air of elated sacredness carried on through the pregnancy, even though Tomas was absent for most of it. "He'll come back," Blythe said, and didn't see any point in spending energy worrying herself. That's what she had told Marion. To Marion, it seemed as though Blythe had come to a precipice – and jumped. And now she was flying. Marion had never been good at those kinds of leaps, but she had the sense she could muster the courage to leap for Blythe's tail feathers.

Marion cooked her creamy fettuccine alfredo, the only thing Blythe could stomach, for dinner four weeks straight then bought pastel-coloured baby socks, a plush white bunny. She massaged Blythe's shoulders, sponged vomit off the bathroom tiles, drove her to doctors appointments, and held the ultrasound photograph in her trembling hands, silently hoping Blythe was wrong about Tomas.

Overnight, Blythe was nine months along. Tomas reappeared. He had a new job as a foreman and had bought a cabin an hour up the coast with one bedroom, a porch, and a tiny garden. The kitchen was freshly painted cherry blossom pink. "I bought it for the nursery," he explained. "Then realized we don't know the gender yet – though I feel that she's a she." Within a week, Blythe and all the things that Marion had shared with her for four years were cleared out of the apartment.

Marion woke early the next morning. Rain flecked against her window. The purple house had come with a four-poster bed which she had layered with quilts found in the closet. She was the baked apricot inside a millefeuille, she said to herself, in this bed. All of the furnishings belonged to the landlady. Marion had never met her, simply arranged a rental agreement over the phone, and then arrived to a key left in the mailbox.

Most mornings, in the winter, Marion woke to a mist pressing against the window, crystally opaque. The locals called it "ice fog." It blotted out whatever weak, silvery sunlight might try to pass through. In a way, Marion liked the ice fog, or at least found a kind of comfort in the crystals. In some compartment of her mind, she imagined the fog was a gauze being wrapped around her life; she was a pearl earring in a plume of cotton batten. She felt no one could possibly reach her through this fog. Though she understood, in another compartment, that that was not how reality worked, she used the fog to explain the lack of phone calls.

Now that it was June, a dry, hard spring wind that had stripped away the snow, had torn at the ice fog, too. Beyond her window the grey was translucent; she could see the corner of her neighbours' rooflines and understood that there were other people nearby.

Marion flexed her ankles and began to swish her legs along the cotton sheets, making a kind of sheet-angel; then she lay very still. So still that she decided she was about to calcify. It had happened before. She made her arms move, peeled back each quilt.

Blythe had asked that Marion be present for the home birth, but, at the last moment, had arranged for Marion to stay instead at a neighbour's – Tomas wanted it to be just the two of them for the first days. Marion slept at the neighbour's, but walked across the yard to Blythe's for every meal as soon as she realized that Tomas could not be relied on to make anything beyond canned soup and ham sandwiches with too much mayonnaise.

The baby arrived as a tidal wave of new emotion and meaning and purpose, and if Tomas minded Marion's presence, he lost his train of thought before speaking it to her, in a haze of exhausted awe. Blythe looked pale, but ecstatic with the tiny brownish-pink baby in her arms. Her eyes had a wild look and then they would glaze over, becoming intensely steady. She spoke in whispers over the baby's head, as though afraid to break the spell they were all under.

Marion sat on the edge of the bed. An hour might pass and she would not have moved away, just watching the little body rise and fall, asleep on her dozing mother's breast. Once Blythe opened an eye and saw Marion there. Her smile was full of sleep. "Did you know, Mare," she asked, "that babies learn to regulate their breathing by matching it to their mother's breathing?"

Marion could only shake her head. Blythe lifted the baby gently and laid her, curled and warm, onto Marion's chest. "Hold her while I go to the bathroom?"

She sat there, never so aware of her own breathing, of how deeply important it was, how beautiful, and how uncomplicated. It was as though, at this late age, life was showing her a magic trick she'd never been aware of, had never known she could perform, if she chose to. It seemed unfair that she had been kept from this important secret for so long, until it was almost too late. Marion startled when Blythe came back into the room;

when she peeled the baby from Marion's chest it felt as though she had stripped a line of duct tape off the pink tissue of Marion's heart. It left a raw stripe.

After getting out of bed and dressing, Marion went to the kitchen. She poached an egg, swirling the whites gently so that it lay neatly when she spooned it onto her plate. She was tearing basil leaves from the stalk when she heard a loud bang at the door and someone called: "Halloo!"

Then his head was in the door, peering down the hallway. "Didn't forget about me, did ya?"

Marion's eyes widened, but otherwise she remained composed. "No, of course not. Would you like an egg?"

Derek swung his arm up and dangled a silver lunch pail. "Got everything we need right here."

She looked down at her egg. She wanted to press into it with her fork. The yolk would ooze out slowly with just the right consistency, she knew it. Watching a perfect yolk spill onto a white plate was one of her small daily pleasures. It was hard to get the yolk just right – everyone had their favourite texture, and Marion was best at poaching Blythe's to perfection. Blythe had once called her The Poached Egg Whisperer.

She looked at Derek, took in his beige coveralls and smile. The little earring caught the light in the hallway. A glint. She brushed the basil from her hands. "Let me just get my sweater."

Marion looked out the window as Derek drove and talked. He had his window down, elbow angled out, gesturing with his broad hand as they passed scrub and rock that, to her, looked indecipherable. "This one," he said, "is where you can find wild blueberries come September, and over there's a bog full of high-bush cranberries – sweeter than low-bush, though they smell like wet dog." Leaning to look over the edge of the road, she saw they were climbing a steep crevasse.

He slowed the truck, and craned his neck toward her window.

"Old riverbed," he said.

She saw stripes in the jagged rock, darkening the further down they rippled. "What's underneath?"

His shoulder hitched as he geared the truck into park. "Clay, permafrost, rock. Probably marbled with some quartz, or possibly copper. Root and rot. The usual, I guess. You looking for gold?"

She frowned, puzzled, and he laughed.

"You really aren't the typical tourist, are you? The whole city's built on gold – you know that, right? Gold's what lured the settlers up."

"Yes, of course," she said, vaguely offended. "I just – I'm not that interested in gold."

"Well, what are you interested in?"

She peered back down into the crevasse, tried to articulate what it was she was trying to see there. "Where I'm from is so green. There's so much soil. But I think, *just* soil. You can dig it up. Here, it's like all these layers of tissue. Permanent tissue. The past hardens and stays."

He was watching her, and grinned. "Not so hard as you think – you can blast it apart, and it shifts around all the time, too. That down there's a perfect example: a slice into the past, as you say, but look – in some places the permafrost has risen to the top, rock has fallen down below. I can take you down there sometime and give you a closer look."

She found herself shaking her head.

He seemed offended, so she said: "It kind of scares me."

He looked at her a moment, smiled a softer smile, then shifted the gear back into drive. "It's just minerals and time, Marion."

As the days passed, Marion became unsure where to stand in the tiny cabin with Tomas present, so she gravitated to the kitchen to whip up thick soufflés, fry fish in butter and panko, pour brownie batter into pans. She grilled pink steaks and tore lettuce leaves and slathered them in creamy dressing. She broke off squares of good chocolate and left them on tiny plates at Blythe's bedside. All the foods she imagined Blythe needed to get her strength back and produce milk. Blythe ate hungrily and the baby nursed hungrily and then, after two weeks, Tomas began clearing his throat whenever Marion approached the mother and baby. He coughed when she spoke. Still, she would have stayed longer, unable to imagine not seeing Lila for days at a time, but Blythe told her it was all right, Tomas just needed some time without a guest in the house, then she could come back. She'd call. Marion filled the fridge with bone broth, custard, and carrot-ginger-orange juice, then drove back to Victoria alone.

At first there were daily, then weekly, phone calls. Marion sat eating popcorn, listening to Blythe over the speakerphone. She couldn't get enough of Blythe's revelations. She asked, "What is she doing now? Can you send a picture?"

"I feel she came to us, not just through me, but through some other place, like some kind of spiritual threshold. Like, just when we were on the verge of settling for something less, she emerged as this possibility, this chance, for something more. Does this make any sense?" Blythe laughed into the phone. She wasn't one to use words like "spiritual threshold" and seemed both amused and fascinated by her new way of thinking. "She was already this soul, this being, who came here with an offering. She chose us."

In the apartment in Victoria, the one they had previously shared, Marion sat on the floor. "Yes, wow. That's exactly what it feels like. She found us."

On the other end, Blythe cleared her throat. "Tomas and me, I meant." There was a quick pause. "I have to go, Mare. I'll call you later."

But it didn't happen. Lila turned two months old, then five months. Marion kept an overnight bag packed in case Blythe should call. After a long communication drought, Blythe emailed about a first birthday party. Marion baked vanilla cake with ganache and wrote Lila's name in looping lavender spirals. She pressed tiny violet petals into the ganache in the shape of a heart. She carefully packed it in the cake-sized Tupperware she had bought just for the occasion, but Blythe called at the last minute to say a visit was not going to work.

They didn't have to drive far to Fish Lake. In the air, she smelled the grassy sweetness of newly opened buds. He had a faded red rowboat and several complicated-looking rods.

"They're not so hard to use," he said, handing her one. At first there was a quiet flurry of preparation. Musty orange life preservers dug up and brushed off, the boat sliding into the water, tipping under her weight then righting itself, the tackle box rummaged through for bait and hooks. The boat smelled like a garage – earthy, masculine. He talked all the while: about the fish, the lake, his favourite aunt. He talked the way people who love to talk do, with great enthusiasm for his own tales and a rising and falling cadence that often ended in a crescendo. Each small story spilled into the next one. She could hear exclamation points punctuating his swooping strings of words.

"Not much of a talker, are you?" he said suddenly, cutting the tail off his own story.

Marion was holding a rod with both hands. It was cool for June, so he'd insisted on draping his canvas coat around her shoulders. The coat had a comforting smell and warmth, and Marion realized she felt somewhat at ease out on this boat with this man, despite the strangeness of being out on a boat, with this particular man. Fishing.

"No. I guess I'm not," she said.

He grinned. "What say we have some brunch?"

She glanced at the lunch pail, imagining salami sandwiches with fakely yellow mustard or some other artificial, unpalatable thing.

"I'm not all that hungry," she said, then spotted his thermos rolling on its side by his foot. She thought she could tolerate bad coffee for one morning. "Maybe just coffee for me."

"Oh, this isn't coffee. Don't drink it when I fish. Makes me too jittery. You really have to be in the zone when you fish. The

Zen-zone, I call it. Here, let me pour you some." He reeled in his line and tucked the hook into an eye on the rod, slipped the handle into a notch. It was all done gracefully and efficiently. When he twisted the Thermos lid off, she watched his hands. Squarish fingernails with dashes of black earth under them – sign of a gardener. A scuffed class ring.

"Where did you go to school?" she asked.

"Didn't. Dropped out of high school. This is my dad's. We didn't get along so well, but he gave me this. He's off in the bush somewhere." He turned to the shore and she, following his look, had a mental flash of an old man, mean-looking, crouched behind a bush, sitting there, waiting.

"I don't mean there," Derek said with some disgust, catching her gaze. "I mean the bush at large."

"I know," she said defensively. She realized she was frowning at his ring, and he was watching her. "Don't you find it hard to wear it?"

He held up his hand and took a long look at the ring. "Nah. He's not in there. And anyway, I sorted through all that. I wear it to remind myself to never be an asshole – 'specially if I ever have kids."

He groped around in a cloth bag and came up with a blue enamel mug. Then he poured something steaming into it. She smelled cocoa. He passed it to her.

Marion hooked a finger through the handle and felt the cup's warmth seep into her palm. She dipped her nose into the steam. "This is good chocolate."

Derek nodded, pleased. "Eighty per cent," he said. "Single origin bean."

She laughed lightly, not expecting "single origin bean" to come out of his mouth. There was a slight challenge in his tone, though he didn't look at her.

All right, she thought. "Where's it from?"

He looked clearly pleased. "You tell me."

She took a sip, let it pool in her mouth and lie thickly on her tongue. She tasted plum. At the edges, just a touch of mushroomy earthiness. It was bright. Zippy. She closed her eyes and swallowed slowly. She had to let the outer layers wear away to get to the very centre, that was the secret of tasting well. If you crushed the centre with your teeth, the chocolate got mashed together, and lost the core. There. "Madagascar – a Valrhona," she said, opening her eyes.

Derek was rapt, eyes wide. He clapped two hands over his heart. "I knew it! I knew it the first time I saw you at Shelly's. You bought that really good Dick Taylor bar. Do you remember that?"

She furrowed her brow. "Well, I remember buying it. You were watching me?"

"Hell, yes," he said, showing his teeth. "There are exactly three people in town besides Shelly and me who eat the good stuff. I know who they are because sometimes we have chocolate tasting nights. You should come!"

"Maybe," Marion said. He looked disappointed and she had to turn away. His emotions, playing on his face too clearly, made her embarrassed for him. She could hear her critique to Blythe: too enthusiastic, too forward, and besides, how could it make sense? A man like him loving those rare chocolates that tasted of the earth they were born from.

It went quiet in the boat and Marion snuck a sideways look at him. She waited for him to start up his talking again, but he didn't. She shifted on the hard, wooden seat, and let her eyes move briefly to his face. "I just don't know how much longer I'll be here," she said. He was looking out at the water, appearing to concentrate on his line.

"Not much of a fisher," she said after a moment, her voice thin. He looked at her, wounded, and she blinked rapidly. "I meant me."

"Oh. Well, that's true." He began reeling in his line calmly.

She coughed. "I like it here."

"Yeah, it's a good lake."

"I mean the Yukon."

He didn't take his eyes off the line. "Do you, now?"

She coughed again, a little clearing of her throat. "I do. It's just different than what I expected. I thought I'd love the landscape – the mountains and the northern lights and all that. I don't, though. If you look at the landscape as a big picture, it's pretty harsh." She laughed, but the laugh didn't sound like her. "But I like the rocks." She flushed, thinking she sounded stupid. "I like that people seem settled here, rooted. A lot of the people I know back home are less attached. They come and go. I didn't think they would. I didn't know how it easy it would be for me to leave until I did. I don't necessarily want to feel that way..." She swallowed.

He looked at her out of the corner of his eye.

"People are always saying you should let go, but I think it's good to be attached to something if it – if it means a lot to you." She looked down. "That's all."

She fiddled with her fishing rod. The reel was jammed.

"Like this," he said, taking it from her and whirring it around in a slow circle. "Want me to cast for you?"

She nodded and watched him press a thumb to the line, arch his arm back and release. She found it a beautiful motion. A gossamer thread ribboned through the cotton sky, then there was the sound of water being kissed and she could trace the line squiggling back to the rod, to his hand, his arm, his body. He passed it to her carefully.

"People are always saying you should let go, huh?" He said, and she flushed again.

"I mean, in general. People say that."

"Sure."

"Do you think you'll always live here?" she asked.

"I belong to it."

She looked at him in surprise, waited for him to explain, but he didn't, and then she realized he didn't have to.

"You love it."

He nodded.

She found a life jacket to cushion her. "You said at the choir party that people up here are abandoned or banished, but that's not true for everyone. Some people have always been from here."

He squinted at her. "You mean First Nations?"

"If you've always been from here, and your ancestors have, too, how can you be forgotten about?"

He shifted forward, rooted around in his back pocket and came out with a toothpick, which he stuck in his mouth. He swapped the pick from one side to the other. She thought he was probably not going to answer her question and for a moment she feared she'd said something inadvertently offensive.

He was scratching his neck. "I guess there are lots of ways, large and small, to be hung out to dry," he said.

"I guess so." They sat in silence.

Marion thought of the weight of Lila in her arms, the same heaviness as a small bag of sugar. She thought of her eyelids, a light violet sheen, almost translucent. How impossibly faint her fingernails were, just the tiniest dab of tissue.

"Somebody hung you out down there?" Derek asked. She didn't respond, and then in her mind, she could re-hear it as a statement and there was no need to reply.

She cleared her throat. "What's in the lunch pail?"

He had made spring rolls with slivers of bright carrot and shining glass noodles. He unscrewed a small jar of red sauce that had delicate hoops of orange chili peppers floating on top. She bit into a spring roll and tasted pea sprouts, ginger. A larger jar held pad Thai, still hot and smelling of tamarind, lemongrass, fish sauce. It was a meal that exploded in tiny bursts in her mouth. Miniature spicy fireworks. He didn't talk when he ate and he held the spring rolls delicately, took small bites, so small for his mouth.

I think you need to let go, Mare. The last thing Blythe had said. Where do you fall to when you let go of the only thing that's holding you in place? I already know what's at the centre of my heart, Marion thought to herself: a pale pink wound, the exact size and shape of a mother and her baby.

Afterwards, he drove her home. He had caught two grayling and she had caught nothing.

"I'm going to fry these up tonight," he said. "Maybe make a Caesar salad to go with." She waited, but he didn't invite her.

She knew a Riesling that would go well with that, she thought. If she wanted to, she could find him. Stop by Shelly's first. If not tonight, then another night.

"I work for a mining company," he said suddenly. "Since you asked. Drill down to test sites. Environmental safety crew. Mostly I climb down holes."

"Oh." She nodded at him. "That's good."

His face shifted into a sort of half-smile, and then she realized this smile of his was a kindness. She was suddenly aware of her awkwardness, and that he was smiling, made her soften into it.

"Do they – do they tie you to something so you don't fall?"

"Nah. I got a good grip." She searched his eyes to see if he was serious. Yes. He turned and looked out his window, his knee jiggling. She thought he was maybe waiting for her to get out of his truck, so she moved quickly for the door and pulled on the handle.

"It must take a lot of courage. To do what you do." Before he could respond, she slid from the front seat, feeling like a child to be so high up and have to fetch around with her toes for the ground. She turned and raised a hand and he did the same, smiled with his mouth closed, his eyes on hers, and drove off.

She walked through the grass of her yard. It was so scrubby and dry she could hear it crackle underfoot.

The phone was ringing in the kitchen. She ran to it and said hello breathlessly. It was the first time she'd received a call on this line. She heard someone breathing.

"Blythe?" she asked softly.

"Elaine," a male voice said. "Is that you, Elaine?"

The voice had only the slightest inflection; it barely warranted a question mark. It was a low voice, issued from deep in the belly, not from the nose.

"No. No, I'm sorry," Marion said. She paused. The voice on the other end said nothing but did not hang up. She could hear steady breathing. She didn't want him to hang up. Her eyes fetched around her kitchen. "I'm just renting for the year. Maybe Elaine lived here before."

Still, just the breathing. "Maybe I could find some kind of contact information for you, so you can – so you can reach her," she said and opened a kitchen drawer, closed it. She scanned the fridge door, but she knew there was nothing.

"I'm looking for Elaine," the voice rumbled.

Marion nodded. "I know," she said. "I'm so sorry."

She went to the purple chair in the corner of the kitchen and sat down, the cord tugging from the wall. She held the phone tightly. She listened to him breathe and didn't speak. She listened and found her breath matching his. It would only last a few seconds, she knew, but she wished it could go on longer. Then she took her own breath.

"She doesn't live here anymore," she said. There was a shuffling sound, a soft hand passing over his speaking end of the phone, another in-breath. She reached up and pulled down on the receiver with a finger. There was a click. She let the phone drop to her chest and cradled it there a moment before placing it back on the receiver.

ACKNOWLEDGEMENTS

Thank you: to my agent Stephanie Sinclair, for being a source of kindness and clarity. To Janet Somerville, Barry and Michael Callaghan, for your fine eyes for detail and your excitement in these stories. Thank you to my children's grandparents, whose loving care of my children allowed me precious pockets of time in which to write. Thank you to my Yukon writing group, Jamella and Kirsten, who read the early drafts of these stories, and to my classmates and professors at the University of British Columbia who inspired and guided me: Miriam Toews, Heather O'Neill, Anosh Irani, Alix Ohlin, and many more.

Thank you, dear husband.

Thank you Ontario, the Yukon, Nova Scotia, British Columbia, and Michigan for preoccupying me so.

I am fortunate to have many incredible people in my life who have shown me, all along, the rich complexity and beauty of the lives of girls and women: my mother, Jan; my grandmother, Neva; my sisters, Sarah and Carrie; my aunts Odie, Becky, Julie, Bunny, and Marilyn; my Bash aunts Carolyn, Mandy, Sharrie, Kathleen, Sarah, Pam, and Peggy; my Zdybel cousins and Bash sisters; my friends Kate, Line, Janice, Brynne, Clare; and my "bosom friend," Celina.

In addition to appreciating them for the time and inspiration they've provided, I'd like to also thank my parents, sisters, family, and best friend for knowing me as a writer – for always considering me as one, for never once doubting or diminishing my dream – from childhood on. I'm profoundly grateful to you; I offer you the best of me.

GRANTS, PROGRAMS, AWARDS, AND PUBLICATIONS

This collection of stories was written with generous support from the Canada Council for the Arts.

The author received editorial advice and guidance for this collection through The Excelsis Group/BMO Financial Group Mentoring Program.

The collection was shortlisted for the HarperCollins/UBC Prize for Best New Fiction.

"The Critics" won the annual $10,000 Carter V. Cooper Short Fiction/Emerging Writer Award. "Honey Maiden" was short-listed for the same award.

"The Last Thunderstorm Swim of the Summer" appeared in *The New Quarterly* (and was winner of their Peter Hinchcliffe Short Fiction Award).

"Northern Tether" appeared in *The Malahat Review*, Issue 213.

"House Calls" appeared in *The Antigonish Review*, Volume 49, Nos. 197-98.

"Progressive Dinner" appeared online at *PrairieJournal.org*.

"The Critics" and "Honey Maiden" appeared in both the *Carter V. Cooper Short Fiction Anthology: Book Nine* (*CVC9*) and *EXILE Quarterly*, Volume 43, No. 4.

"The Last Thunderstorm Swim of the Summer" was a publisher's nomination for the Writers' Trust Journey Prize, and "Honey Maiden" for a National Magazine Award.

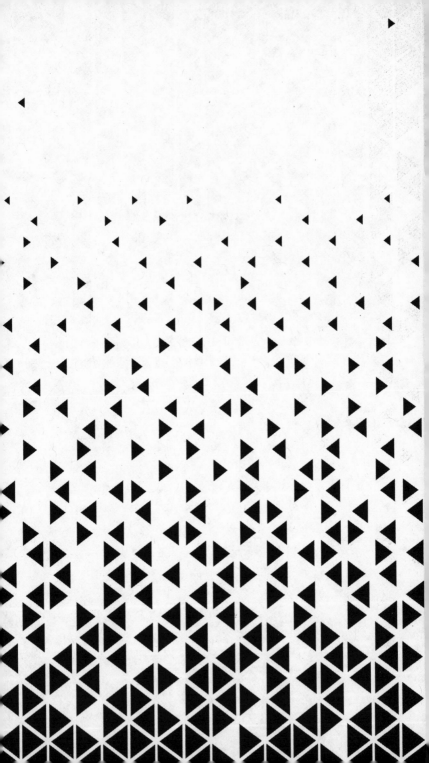